THE BOY KING'S TALE

As told by

Geoffrey Chaucer

Michael January

Winged Lion Publications

Winged Lion Publications

Copyright 2023 by Michael January
All rights reserved under International
and Pan-American Copyright Conventions.

Library of Congress Cataloging on Request
ISBN-13: 978-0-9985663-3-7

Praise for The Boy King's Tale

"Steeped with fast-paced betrayal, intrigue and intense
conflict within an authentic setting, The Boy King's Tale
intermingles historical details with striking and
tantalizing character portraits that give it an edge."
Publishers Weekly BookLife Prize

"A story redolent with intrigues, battles, and
psychological warfare, beautifully written.
For anyone that loves tales of knights, derring-do,
and chivalry, a fantastic read but also for
anyone who just enjoys a rollicking good story!"
Reader's Favorite

"It's difficult to pull off believable vocabulary for stories set
in this time frame, especially in the dialogue,
here accomplished beautifully."
Page Turner Awards

"With vivid descriptions, authentic language, and
characters to root for, this is a great story!
Baker's Book Services

"The characters come alive on the pages with real human
emotions. A remarkable must-read historical novel!"
Historical Fiction Company

"An entertaining, well-written account of a time long ago."
Kirkus Reviews

Other Books by Michael January

Fiction

Secret Memoirs of Mary Shelley: Frankenstein Diaries
Aces: A Novel of Pilots in WWII

Non-Fiction

Favorite Castles: England and Wales
Favorite Castles: More England and Wales
Favorite Castles: Ireland and Northern Ireland
Favorite Castles of Switzerland
Favorite Castles of Germany
Favorite Cathedrals & Churches of Germany

Beware cruel judgment's fate,
any who enter by Traitor's Gate.

PROLOGUE

25th Day of June, 1377

Somber bells rang from the great tower of the Abbey of Westminster as the grey clouded sky suddenly filled with fluttering doves. The doors of the cathedral fairly bulged with London's citizens. Peasants, merchants and tradesmen alike, all dewy eyed, if not weeping outright, pressed in lines into the church, made open for all on this sad day.

A man of middle age in a noble's cloak pushed himself through the crowd from inside the church doors. He limped on a gouty foot and leaned for support on a crooked walking staff. He had raised himself from a lowly station to the court of kings by his skill with

1

words, but on this day, he felt as if all his words had left his mind for the pain of loss. He was soon recognized and quickly surrounded by a small crowd. He knew few of them had skill of letters but his aged days had been filled with recounting his stories at court to those far above their station. Finally, a merchant's son, a boy of fourteen, ventured forward timidly.

"Good sir, will you—speak to us," the boy asked, overcoming his awe at the famous old man. "Tell us, please, one of your tales. A cheerful story would lighten our hearts."

A wheelwright in his leather apron spoke up from the back of the group, "Yes, good sir Chaucer, give us one of your Tales of Canterbury. Tell us the Innkeeper's Tale."

The merchant's son argued for another, "No, kind sir, please spin the Miller's Tale, for I have heard it is merry."

Geoffrey Chaucer, no noble title to his name but Royal Court Poet, so anointed by his sovereign king, looked into the waiting faces. He was warmed by the eager eyes of the youngest of them. He searched his mind for the words to one of his popular stories, but what came to him instead was the present mood of the day. He glanced to the tower of the great church from which he had come and where, even now, his patron lay among a bed of flowers. He spoke to the son of the merchant, reminded by his young age of the subject upon his mind.

"You do prevail upon me. I will indeed tell a tale," said Chaucer. "Yet, this solemn day is not occasion for the mirth of a whimsical parable. Nay, I will tell thee a true tale. It is a story of bloody deeds and villainous intrigues." He tousled the head of the youngest of them, with a smile, "Yet, fear not for unsettled sleep, for it may also be a story of great joys."

The poet eased himself to sit on the steps. The crowd gathered around him, to better hear as he began to bind his story spell.

"This shall be the Boy King's Tale," intoned the teller of stories, "for 'tis indeed the story of a boy who was made king, at an age not much junior to your years, young Master." He rested a kind hand, cramped and wounded by the long holding of quills on the shoulder of the son of the merchant. "Yet, listen near, for though a crown may make a king, a man must truly make himself."

"I will begin," he spoke with a cadence to draw in his listeners, "with that fateful night whence all our lives would be decided."

"When we would be free or slave?" asked the Merchant's son, eagerly, knowing the legend.

Chaucer smiled with a weighty nod, "Free by the rule of law and not enslaved to capricious overlord,

3

which indeed was the choice on balance. It was a damp November in the Year of our Lord, Thirteen Hundred and Thirty, when a Parliament of Lords and Commons had been summoned to Nottingham, their numbers from far-spread shires of the land gathered in the fields outside the city walls."

~~~

CHAPTER ONE

1

4:20 AM
18th Day of November, 1330

The impregnable walls of Nottingham Castle stood on a rocky promontory above the encampment, pushing up from the surrounding thick forests like a cancerous mole. Below the fortress cliffs, in the shadowed meadows surrounding the hamlet of Nottingham, tents emblazoned with the colors and coats-of-arms of gathered English Lords crowded the field. Most of the tents were darkened as brooding night crept across the field, but a few fires were burning late as a drizzling mist fell upon them.

The quiet was broken with a shout of men in one of the tents. A messenger emerged from it to leap on a waiting horse, galloping through the tents soaked with the morning dew toward the castle road. He urged his horse up the steep, rain splattered road to the castle, the animal snorting with the effort, hooves slipping in the mud and clattering across the drawbridge. The messenger ducked under the points of the raised portcullis, thrilled with an inner sense of his part in destiny.

"Missive for the king! News for the king!" he shouted as he reined his horse to a halt. The beast's hooves clattered on the cobblestones, echoing among the battlements, enough to awake any who might have fallen into slumber on this fateful morn.

The bull-like shape of a knight stepped from the shadows to greet the eager messenger, waiting for the news he possessed. Sir John Monmouth, with eyes of stone, snared the reins of the nervous horse in his gauntleted fist, fully encased in his armor as if ready for urgent action when in the pre-dawn darkness all else would be abed.

"What is your news?" Monmouth asked with somber expectation.

The messenger dismounted his animal with excited agitation, sure the news he held would bring gladness to the castle.

"I have tidings for His Grace from the Lords gathered in Parliament," he said breathlessly, expecting to be taken directly to give his report.

"Does the decision fall in the king's favor?" asked Monmouth.

The messenger held his secret for a moment, unsure whether he might give it to any of the household beyond the king himself. But his joy was too much. "Aye! In his favor!" he exclaimed, thrusting the soaked parchment with signatures of the great lords upon it, so that the king's knight might see.

Monmouth ripped the parchment from his hand and held it out toward a darkened archway, where a figure was concealed in the shadows. The messenger squinted uncertainly from the knight to the man in the shadow, but who it was, he could not make out.

"Is it not happy news?!" the eager herald asked with a bright expectation of agreement.

The figure in the shadows only nodded to Monmouth, and the knight smiled darkly.

"Aye. Happy news it is, then," he said with a mirthless grunt, then suddenly wrapped the horse's rein around the messenger's throat and yanked him off the ground in his powerful fist. His feet kicked in futile struggle for life's breath as he was lifted from the ground by the strong knight. The young herald's eyes bulged as he struggled for breath, remembering for a moment his joy at being appointed to court to serve his king, before the light vanished forever. Finally, he was still and Monmouth dropped the limp body to the cobblestones.

"What now, my lord Earl?" Monmouth inquired of his master in the darkness. The moonlight cut across the glistening eyes of the man in the shadows, one orb of darker reflection than the other.

"Seal the gates," he ordered in a voice of calm certainty, deep and sonorous, yet a slight recognizable west country lilt, then turned and strode away across the courtyard.

Monmouth signaled to the keeper of the gatehouse above. Following the command, the gatekeeper released the locking lever and the heavy oak spikes of the portcullis dropped in rattling march down the opening maw. Heavy chains clanked as the drawbridge was raised, with moss covered planks rising above the chasm until the bridge slammed with a heavy thud against its stops.

2

A handsome and fair young man, just eighteen, sat up in bed with a start at the distant sound. He threw back the fur blanket and padded, naked and lean, to a narrow lead-paned window in the thick stone wall. He thrust it open and peered out into the cold night. The waning moon shone over the forests, with no hint yet of the sun, as if no other days may come. Below in the meadow, all seemed quiet, save for a few torches still glowing among the tents. He wondered if they were awake at all, or had they drifted into a sleep of wine and mead with no answer for him.

A young page boy scrambled from his straw mat in the corner at his master's stirring. He quickly gathered the thick ermine-lined suede robe and held it out. Edward, for that was the fair young man's name, wrapped it loosely about himself, and his first notice of the chill was when the fur enfolded him, still yet to warm.

The page scurried to a side table and picked up a wooden box, carved with the symbol of three lions on the hinged top. He brought it to his master as if he might want it as well, for surely this day was the occasion for it. Edward looked at the box, feeling almost as if it was a foreign thing, not belonging to him and even now doubtful of his worthiness. He ignored it and strode with decision to the chamber door, throwing open the solid wooden plank with a disdainful thud against the stone wall.

Left alone with the box, the page decided to risk a peek. He had looked upon the object it held before but was never allowed to touch it. With wondrous awe, he gingerly opened the latch and carefully raised the lid, revealing inside the gleaming gold circle set with jewels, the crown of the King of England. The round, smooth, deeply colored gem stones glistened even in the dark, catching the light of the slash of moon through the window arch. The page wondered if he might dare to touch it. He longed to feel the smooth hardness of the gold. If his master could have been anointed king as a boy not much older than himself, could he not also dream? He thought of putting it on his own head, but quickly the temptation faded, for he knew from close observation of his master the weight of wearing such a thing.

Edward hurried down a cramped spiral stone stair, around and around from his living chamber apartments to the great hall. He strode across the length of the hall to the closed doors at the far end. He pulled at them, but they were held fast, locked. Still, he banged his fist on the wood and rattled them, but to no use. An old man scuffled in, still in bed clothes, aroused by the noise. Edward watched him shuffle unsteadily across the wooden parquet and wondered to himself if he might have to find a new Chamberlain soon.

"By whose command have these doors been sealed, Chamberlain?" Edward demanded.

"The Earl of March, Your Grace," was the answer, the old Chamberlain hesitant as if he might be scolded. "Your mother holds the keys." He bent close to the boy king's ear in a hushed whisper, as if he might be included in the gossip, "'Tis rumored there is a plot by some of the barons below—"

He trailed off under Edward's searing glare. "I know of only one plot here about, Chamberlain—it hatches above in my mother's bedchamber."

The Chamberlain was shocked by his master's boldness, but thought it best to say nothing more, not wishing to ignite the young king's ready temper.

"Has there been an answer from Parliament?" Edward asked, impatient.

"No, my lord. No word has come."

"Is the door to my chapel unlocked—or does God plot against me as well?"

"Shall I arouse your Confessor, Sire?" the Chamberlain asked, hoping to be at least of service.

Knowing the old lord would take the age of man to reach the chapel above, or might even die upon the many steps to it, Edward turned from him and headed back to the stairs, leaving him in mid-sentence.

3

As Edward hurried toward his private chapel, he hesitated at a corridor, lost for a moment in the unfamiliar fortress, as they had only come to Nottingham for the parliament. A sturdy young man of nineteen hurried from the other direction, still in his nightshirt. His brow was furrowed with worry. Edward was glad to see his friend, Richard of Bury. Scarcely more than a year older than he, Richard had been his tutor for the past four difficult years, but at this moment, they both sensed they may have reached the darkest of all.

Richard was short of breath, having been up and down stairs. "Edward, they've boxed us in!" he said urgently. "The locks have been changed. Even the castellan has no keys."

Edward knew already. "Mother keeps them under her pillow."

"What do we do?"

Edward clapped his friend on the shoulder, urging him, "See if we have any allies trapped with us. And we may need weapons."

"What of you?"

Edward could hear the distant cry of an infant drifting from the chamber apartments in the labyrinth of stone above, his attention caught by the sound, feeling a mixture of pride and foreboding.

"I must be a husband." He smiled at the thought of the one pleasure left to him untainted by the intrigue which had brought him to this moment. He braced Richard upon his shoulder and left him to his urgent task.

Edward threw open the door of a sleeping chamber and entered to find Philippa in her fur bed robe holding their baby suckling at her breast. The infant bit too hard and Philippa, a golden-haired girl of seventeen with a warm eternal sweetness, let out a small cry. She then offered a twinkled-eyed smile to her husband. "Your son is as passionate as his father," she said.

"My lord is bold to enter my lady's chamber without knock or announce," said a stern shaky voice from the inner closet. The young queen's Waiting Maid, Lea, appeared with some linens for the babe, though with her aged prune face, she could truly only be called a maid in jest. It was not the first time she had scolded the boy king, unafraid of his position and too well familiar with his moods. Her sharpness with him only hid the deep care she held for the young couple. If only her life had been blessed by their love, she often had wished.

"Where is our guard?" she demanded. "There are clever doings about in this cold, horrid northern country, and you would leave my lady unprotected?"

Edward stroked his son's head tenderly, his heart full with wonder at the miracle, feeling the soft tufts of golden fleece, until Lea wrested the baby from his wife's arms to lay it in the crib. He keenly felt at that moment as if all might be taken from him, for he knew well the perilous balancing point upon which they all stood. He was worried, too, that there had been no sentry posted at the door. But he didn't want to add to their concern.

"And so, is son stolen from the father," he said, as he watched the servant bind his infant first born in swaddling. He dwelt for a moment on thoughts of his own absence from his father, kept separated from him on the cause of his mother's hatred, and from it the cause of their current state. But he could not allow the rising emotions to overcome him and forced his mind to the present danger, not wanting to reveal too much, lest he frighten them.

"The guards have been dismissed," Edward said, as if it were only a matter of detail.

Philippa pressed close to him as his true worry was well concealed. She tenderly rubbed her leg against his, not yet noticing his mood and full of mischief. She had not seen him for a day with all the important ceremonies with the gathered lords and barons.

"Then, we are in private," she purred. "My lord is welcome to enter his lady's chamber any time he feels the urge. Would he enter tonight she would reward him with most enthusiastic shudderings."

Lea swatted at her mistress's bottom, "Lady! You forget yourself with such talk!"

Philippa smiled with secret thoughts, ignoring the old scold. She allowed the familiarity as Lea had long been as much a mother to her as her own.

"Indeed, I forget myself completely when my husband unsheathes his sword." She teasingly licked his ear, "I might even forget that I am angry with him," then, bit his lobe, just lightly, "for he is an unchivalrous lover to allow the black-eyed ogre to make advance on his wife without reproach. I have had to sup in my own chamber to escape his notice."

Edward noticed the half-eaten plate of food on the night table. An old darkness arose within him at the subject of his enemy, one whom he had once loved.

Lea whispered with old gossip, "It is said his Spanish mother was mad and poisoned his father, but your royal father pardoned her of the crime."

"Shush," hushed Philippa to silence her prattle.

Edward caressed her face, trying not to alarm her but intent on making her obey him this once. "Philippa, listen to me. Do not retire to your own bed tonight. Keep our child with you, and sleep with your maid in her bed."

"What is wrong? Edward?" She now could see his troubled mind, but uncertain of the cause.

"Will you do as I command?"

She was still playful with him, "I would rather sleep in my husband's bed. If he would but command me."

"Your restless husband will neither be in his own bed tonight."

"And whose bed will he be in?" she smirked, wanting to ease him.

He kissed her, as if it might be the last. "For the time present, do as I ask. For my mind's rest—I will sleep in no bed but lay before my God."

4

Candles filled the dim gloom of the bare stone private chapel of Nottingham castle with a Holy light, as if the narrow walls might hold refuge from the dark plots outside. Edward prostrated himself before the altar, laying himself naked, face to the floor, with only his robe covering his body, arms stretched to the sides in cruciform. The icy coldness of the flagstone almost burnt against his skin in penance.

Edward took a moment to recall all that had brought him to this place. He believed he had tried to do good, uncertain of his true sins, even as he tried to find the words to confess them. Yet, honest confession was his intent, and perhaps, he thought, his sins might come to him as he spoke aloud to the walls.

"My Lord and Liege God, I, Edward Plantagenet of Windsor, the third of my name, King of England, Lord of Scotland, Ireland and Wales, Duke of Aquitaine, and rightful claimant to the throne of France, prostrate myself before Thy glory as I came into this world, to freely confess my guilts."

He thought for a moment longer in the silence, trying to frame in his mind what might have brought him to this night, which he well knew could be his last on earth, "Lord, forgive me my sins of vanity and my pride, for perhaps it is these faults which now hold me captive in my own house. Forgive my intemperance—for this, too, I know is a fault."

"Is that all you wish to confess, my son? These are small sins to bring about such an unhappy state." Edward was startled by the voice of a monk he had not seen in the shadows, speaking from the corner of the chapel, where he had halted, apparently not wishing to disturb the young king in his communion with the Father.

Edward realized he was not alone with God, but with an audience. He cast an eye to the monk, sizing him up, but was unfamiliar with this confessor. He traveled with his own, but this cleric was surely an inhabitant of this castle of his cousin.

The monk had an honest and sincere face, a man of middle years, with perhaps a wisdom in the eyes. They held an earnestness not to be found in all of his profession, many who had sought the solitude of the cloister to escape the challenges of a worldly life, and many who had brought the sins of the world into their Order. Upon considering him, Edward decided impetuously that he might place his trust in this confessor. He had few friends close about him, and even if the clergyman was false, his confession was unlikely to reveal any secrets his enemy did not know already. Perhaps a perspective unjaundiced by prior knowledge of his intimate history would give him fresh guidance.

"Then, will you hear my full confess, good Father?

"If you wish it, my lord, I will hear it," said the monk, taking the beads from his cassock of the simple white of St Bernard.

Edward was thoughtfully silent as his confessor waited in patience. The young king seemed reluctant and the monk coughed in polite encouragement, "Wherever you care to begin, Sire."

Edward fixed on a thought, feeling the coldness of the stone, and sat up, pulling the robe about him in modesty. "Then I will begin, good Father, where all lives begin—in naked entrance to this world."

And thus Edward would lay out his life as he knew it, before God and his earthly agent, a stranger to him.

The old storyteller, Chaucer, paused a moment in his tale to catch some phlegm in his throat and to see if his audience was with him. He studied the old faces and the younger among them, all enrapt. He would soon recount the darker nature of the story but wanted them with him.

"Forgive me if I began my story at near the end," he said, hiding his well-intended mischief, "but for better understanding, I will reset the time and place to give full meaning to the events of it. A child or man may only know of his very earliest of years through flashes of disconnected memories, brief images, or haphazard recollection of feelings and sensations with no true recall of the living of them, but a prince royal will hear his life repeated to him over and again in story and song sung as lullaby, with the most intimate details scratched in recorded documents. Those telling the story and repeating the song may serve their own cause in the shaping of it, but it could not be escaped, Edward knew as much of his own life and of his family as any might, and here is what he knew—it was only by violent intervention that his name would be Edward at all."

Chaucer then set about to draw a picture for his audience of the earthly arrival of his subject.

5

4 PM
13th Day of November, 1312

In the chapel of the royal castle at Windsor, a naked newborn infant was held aloft by hands with rich jewels on manly fingers. The babe was dripping wet and bawled as it was lowered again into the christening bath by the hands of Edmund Plantagenet, the Earl of Kent. The brother of the king was four and twenty years of age and perhaps the most handsome of a family bestowed with fair features as well as power, and of more cheerful humor than his brother.

Arrayed around the bath for the ceremony were a collection of royal personages, most in the rich reds and greens of England, though knotted among them, a few in the dark azure blue with Fleurs-de-Lis of France. An aged bishop in gold-lined robe dropped Holy waterlets on the infant's forehead, invoking the Christening, naming him as Edward, as his father before him and his before.

The infant Edward's father, the second Edward, called Caernarfon after the place of his own birth, was also a handsome man, now of six and twenty years. For the ceremony, he was garbed in the full regalia of his office, rich ermine-lined red robe of velvet, with the crown upon his blond head of long straight locks carefully set to curl at the bottom. His mood was serious as he pondered his burdens.

Among the French cousins was his queen, Isabella Capet of France, her beauty striking, of dark-hued, almost black hair against which her slate blue eyes, unusual for her country, stood out with a luminescent glow of the intensity of her spirit. The husband and wife did not stand together in joy at the christening of their firstborn son and heir to the throne but were divided by favor among their relatives. The king, rather instead, stood beside a young French knight, Piers Gaveston, he with a handsome and fine angular face.

It was only the voice of the Prelate which filled the chapel with sound, though unspoken conversation and argument seemed to fill the air loudly with resentment and hatred, barely held in check. The joining of the families of the Plantagenet and the Capet was engineered by the first Edward of England and Isabella's father, Philip, called the Fair of France, to end a generation of violence between two cousin states in the hands of these two families since the ascension of Henry II, and the conflicts of his sons, Richard of the Lionheart and John, the Lackland.

The first Edward, known as legendary Longshanks for his unusual height and determined stride, had been as ferocious and clever a monarch as England had known, who by the power of will and of arms, had joined the lands of the lords of Scotland and Wales to the

English counties in a singular island under one crown, one throne. He had set justice on course and peace upon his land, even if by strength and cunning belonging to a king. His son had been granted his name, and upon his death, his seat and scepter, but somewhere had been left behind his strong will and cleverness.

It was not certain that the new infant prince would receive the name of his father. It was argued by the family of his mother that he be named after the King of France, as a sign of the peace secured by the joining of the houses. This suggestion had been received with a casual acceptance by the king, who was, it must be said, unduly influenced by his friend Gaveston and more acclimated to the French way of manners, but met with a violent reaction from his brother Kent, with a swear that the heir to the English throne would bear a French name over his dead and bleeding body.

This view had been expressed in the form of a dagger suddenly drawn and held to the throat of the queen's cousin, Phillip Valois of Anjou, in the hall of the Westminster Palace. The confrontation had been quelled without the shedding of blood and a new war, but the lords of parliament agreed with the sentiment and had writ a decree that the English heir would always bear an English name. Edmund of Kent and the cousin of Valois had made amends, but Edmund henceforward dare not step foot on French soil without armed protection.

"And so it was through this gentle diplomacy," Chaucer paused for a laugh among the gathered throng of growing number, "that the future king's name was Edward of Windsor and not Phillip." Then, he took upon his face a more somber countenance to bring his audience to the present story. "But the true course of his fate was set, not with a birth, but rather a death, from which all else would fall."

~~~

CHAPTER TWO

1

22nd Day of March, 1322

The stillness of the English wood was broken by the pounding of hooves and snorting of horses under gallop. Ten men rode, whipping their horses toward a boat, waiting to take them in escape across the Irish Sea. They were English lords and barons, some in armor, others in traveling coats. As they rounded a bend in the wavering road, near in sight of the sea, a company of men-at-arms and knights wearing the colors of three lions on red appeared behind them, urging their own horses to pace.

Suddenly, another company of King's Men emerged on the road ahead, blocking the escaping cadre. Among them was a knight in armor with ribbons of the gold and red colors of the House of Despenser. Trapped between the two ranks, swords and mace were drawn, as the horses snorted effort, urged by the masters on their back, the brown earth was churned into the red mud of flowing blood.

In the midst of the melee, among the rebellious lords who had attempted escape from the king's wrath were two aging men, both of the House of Lancaster, Thomas, the Second Earl, and his brother, Henry, who seemed to be the greatest objects of the king's soldiers, surrounded in close guard by the younger knights, who protected them.

The most fiercely fighting of the rebellious knights wore the colors of unicorns on black with hatched yellow chevrons, the Lord of Wigmore, who hacked down man after man with his long sword and strong arm. His efforts were enough that the brothers Lancaster and a small guard could break away. But before they could gain distance, a lance pierced the coat of the elder Earl of Lancaster. The thrust was true and deep as the lance in the side of Our Lord, and in throes of death, the elder earl tumbled from his horse.

"Lancaster! He's killed!" shouted a young baron to Henry of Lancaster.

Only two years younger than his brother, but as grey-bearded as his kin, Henry held his horse to turn to see the leader of his house fallen.

"Brother!" was his only exclamation.

"We cannot stay, my lord!" The young Baron of Montagu at his shoulder urged him to flee.

Henry could not bring himself to move. Would it be cowardice to leave his brother behind and take his title to himself? Could he live with that upon his heart? He held to watch what would become of his brother as they dragged him to sit him up, though he be dead. His head was held by one knight while another raised a sword to cleave through the neck.

As others fell around the strong black-coated knight, he was bashed by the mace of the knight of red and gold colors and knocked from his horse.

The younger barons finally prevailed upon the second Lancaster and they broke away to escape down the road, while the black-coated knight was grappled and captured.

The knight who struck the blow circled on his horse in triumph and raised his visor. It was the lean, and one could even say pretty, face of the king's appointed Exchequer, at two and twenty years, young for his office, Hughes les Despenser. He smiled in a self-satisfied pleasure.

"Voyons l'œil au beurre noir de ce traître, Mortimer de Wigmore," Despenser said with a grin, still clinging in affectation to the French of his Norman ancestors. (Let us see the black eye of this traitor, Mortimer of Wigmore).

The men of the King's guard pulled the helmet from the knight's head, revealing the strong and still handsome face of a man of forty years, with a black, trimmed beard just streaked with grey, Roger Mortimer. He stood his ground and glared up at the favorite of the English king, who still held loyalty to his distant foreign heritage. A gleam of defiance was in his eyes, with one of the irises so dark as to appear black, and spoke with a west county lilt of the Wales borderland, as he would later from the shadows of Nottingham.

"Rather traitor, than a king's mistress—" Mortimer grinned. "Mon petit!"

With an incensed growl, Despenser kicked his spurred foot into the face of the rebel knight.

"Smile, my dear Mortimer," he crooned in a soft voice meant to even confirm the other's taunt, "if you can, with a body absent a head."

2

Ever since King John put his hand to the Great Charter, the question of who had power to rule England, whether King by divine right, or the Lords and Commons in Parliament, had been unsettled. And it was this question at the core of the dispute between the king's cousins of Lancaster and the ruling house of the Plantagenet. It is the nature of men and kingdoms that these questions seem not to matter when times are good. Under the third Henry, who had followed John, and in the golden and bloody victorious times of the first Edward of the house, when lands were gathered by victories on the field and distributed among the lower houses, that loyalty to the king was assured. Since the father's end, however, and the rise of the Second Edward to the throne, victory was no longer a natural expectation as would seem an English birthright. The second Edward, of Caernarfon, was not of a nature suited to the efforts of war. He preferred the pursuits of music and poetry, and the fine clothes of court to the blood and mud of drawn edged steel.

The lands of Ireland were held to the crown by Norman lords who had been given dominion by grant of Henry II, and rebellion had been settled by marriage of his steady arm, Strongbow de Clare, to a daughter of the Irish king. The restless Welshmen had been held in check in conquest, first by the iron will of Edward I and his impregnable iron ring of stone fortresses, then, mollified in the second by his promise that the next king of England would be a son born in Wales and not speak a word of English. This was a promise cleverly made when his queen, Eleanor, then resident in the newly completed Caernarfon Castle was thick with child, and upon his birth, when Christened with the same name as his father, the infant was named as the Prince of Wales, and so the Welsh were settled, if not entirely content.

Yet, the proud and obstreperous lords of the Scots lands were another matter. Edward the father had subdued the rebellious lords of the north with force of battle, but when the second Edward was drawn to hold his father's grip, he had been shown a poor and unwilling commander, with the Scots again enforcing a border at the Battle of Bannockburn where twenty-thousand English knights and men-at-arms had fallen to the heavy Scottish Claymores. A tender peace had been settled on Scottish terms, yet the Stone of Scone, taken by the English king as a sign of dominion, still remained under the English throne at Westminster.

The English lords rankled at their defeat, blaming the king and the wealthy favors of unearned lands and powers he bestowed on his close, and they believed, too intimate friends. They blamed him as well for the way he failed to keep his father's promise to Wales, not speaking English at court, for it was certainly not the melodic lilt of the Welsh language he spoke, but his favor of the French language of his Norman ancestors which offended them still.

The queen he had married to satisfy his father was surely born in that country, but even she had made an effort to win over her new countrymen by speaking its natural language of the commoner. She was beloved of the people for it, and for her beauty, for she was one of the fairest of beauties her land could produce.

It is true that few would see her in the flesh, but it was by the stories that were told by one and repeated by another and sung in songs, that her fame and goodwill had spread among the ordinary people. They had also heard the gossip, which is passed in hushed whispers freely in the drinking halls and gathering wells, that the king, though faithful in his duties as a husband, delivering heirs for the kingdom and spare progeny, had abandoned her in love, even despite her beauty, for the company of his male companions. Thus, the common people felt certain that she did not deserve to be treated so cruelly.

3

The green of the tower fortress of London was busy with activity on a peaceful day. A misty fog had drifted up the River Thames with the tide, but it was not so gloomy as it had been. Children of the household ran and shouted as they chased a rolling hoop across the green below the walls of the White Tower keep and past the chopping block in the yard, still fresh with blood stains streaking its wooden sides. So much blood had soaked into the oak that it was near black on the face of it where the fluid of traitors would run to seek return to the earth below.

Edward, now just thirteen years of age, ran with the others, laughing, exuberant and seeming as care-free as his lessers. He played among them as any other boy might. His younger brother, John, just ten years, also played with them. The children were kin of the guests of the king. The castle was crowded as the royal court was present for the council held at Westminster, but many had come to London for the trials. So many had passed through the gates where boats could enter from the river that it had come to be called the Traitor's Gate.

Edward stopped his running at the chopping block as the others passed it uncaring, but he was held for a moment by the thought of it. He wondered if one day, he too would require men to place their necks upon it, to collect heads to join those even now on pikes on the bridge of London. It was a heavy quandary which consumed his mind. He was the grandson of one mighty king and son of another, and every day knew that same duty would descend upon him. Would he have the will to command that all must obey him, at the price of death? If kings ruled by Divine Right, that the hand of almighty God reached out command to his soul, would he be worthy of that power should it fall upon him?

It was while he was so occupied with such lofty rumination on his promised future that he was hit and knocked to the ground. He had been struck by the flying body of another older boy who had been chasing the hoop and had lost his footing to career into the first prince of the realm. Edward was unharmed but sat upon the ground in his fine rich clothes. He stared up at the other boy, his first mood a quick anger, but tempered by his recent thoughts of bloody executions, as he wiped a trickle of blood from his cheek where he had struck a small stone in the grass.

Richard of Bury stood frozen on the green. He was not frightened for his own fate at the prospect of having decked the royal prince but worried on how his own execution, for which he was surely now at risk, would reflect upon his family. Richard was fifteen, just two years older than the boy prince he had assaulted, and thought it a pity he would not live to see how the world turned out. He offered his hand to the prince to help him rise, and to his surprise, Edward took it and lifted himself to steady on his feet.

"If I were king," Edward said with a sudden grin, "I would knight thee for such a blow. But as I am yet only a prince, I can merely dub thee, friend." He clapped the other boy on the shoulder with an easy comradery as sudden as the blow that had struck him down. "By what name are you called?"

"Richard, of Bury, Highness, in Suffolk."

"Then, from now you shall be Sir Friend Richard." Edward said it with a grin, knowing from the instant they would be friends, for he had the talent of quick assessment. "How do you come to court? From what house?"

"I am the second of my family, Highness. My father is the Lord of Willoughby," Richard explained. "I have come from tutelage at Oxford. My father only thinks me fit for clergy, and I am soon to receive my order."

"A grim priest?" Edward's face screwed in quick thought, as he could be impetuous. "I don't think so. Do you know Latin? My father rhymes in Latin. But I have come to suspect there is something in his verse not meant for my ears." He bent close in a hushed whisper. "Do you know the dirty words?"

Before Richard could answer that he did know some words not found in the Catholic catechism, a soft woman's voice called out with the accent of natural born French.

It was Queen Isabella who had seen her son knocked to the ground. She hurried across the green, leaving her maids behind.

"Edward!" she called in worry, for she doted on him. The queen of the realm was now eight and twenty years, and as fresh in allure as she might ever be. She hurried with silk and velvets flowing.

Richard looked at her approaching. He had only heard of her in excited gossips.

"Is that the queen?! God, she is as beautiful as they all say."

Edward leaned close to whisper before his mother was too near to hear, "I'm told she was more so, before suckling. Now, she fusses over wrinkles."

Richard grew nervous at the approaching famous lady. He stepped a distance away, with a bowed head and dropped to a knee, only to be ignored as Isabella reached her son to fuss over his minor scrape.

"Mon petit. Etes-vous injurer? You bleed." She wiped at the wound with her fine lace kerchief.

Embarrassed to be seen in need of a mother's care, Edward squirmed to shake her off. "Maman! Je suis bien! Stop! I am nearly fourteen!"

His mother dismissed his complaint, licking the kerchief and finishing wiping the wound. Edward caught the amused smirk on Richard's face, trying to keep bowed so the queen might not see.

A royal party emerged from the high keep. Among them was Edward's father, Caernarfon, three years beyond forty now, his long hair and beard already turning to grey strands, which gave him rather the image of a chess piece king. Beside him was Despenser, who wore powder to cover his pox scars in public.

"Father!" Edward called to the king in his crowded company. Isabella tried to hold him, to keep him from her husband, but he broke from her grasp and ran across the courtyard, past the bloody block, to his father, surrounded by his retinue. They had been long separated, with Edward kept to the company of his mother, and he often wondered during this time if it was his father's wish not to see him, or the advisors of his mother who arranged their separation.

"I have not seen you since Witsun," the boy said with eager hope. "When you go hunting in the north, will you take me? I have learned the bow and quarrel." The boy indeed had shown an interest in the arts of weaponry since an early time in his life.

Caernarfon looked at his son's hopeful face, not sure what he might say to the eager boy. His agreement with the queen was that his eldest son should remain in her care with his younger siblings. He was not especially comfortable with the antics and questions of children, and though he was not pleased to enjoy their company, he was sad for the distance just the same.

Edward looked to his father's close companion and advisor, with his fine array more opulent than any others and vain powder on his face. He knew what was said of his father, that he cared for this friend as much or more than he had the buried and hated Gaveston, and certainly more than his queen. He was not sure whether to believe it, or even entirely what it meant, but he did know for certain that his father had raised this man to an exalted station above all others, and kept always at his side, while his son was kept away from him.

Edward had heard the stories of Gaveston, the king's former intimate, long ago beheaded by the anger of the barons, but had not known him. His father had taken favorites to his side against the advise of the heads of great houses who swore to him, and Despenser was as much or more disliked as the former, which caused Edward to study him on the stair as if to understand.

Despenser met the boy's wondering gaze with an absence of the slightest care.

"I want to learn Latin," Edward blurted. "Mother's priests only teach me the Psalter and Hours. I want to understand law, like my grandfather, if I am to serve the people."

Edward Caernarfon smiled, bemused by his son's curious mind. They had been much kept apart by the queen's insistence, but he well knew that his wife's selection of tutors kept his son occupied in arts and languages, and yet even deeper philosophies. She denied him nothing.

"Law is what we decide it to be," the king said with half-serious amusement, repeating an argument he often had with the collection of lords who intended to control him and deny his God granted right.

"It is the people who serve," Despenser added, with a point as sharp as a sword.

Caernarfon reached out with a jewel-ringed hand to touch his son's face and stroke his hair, with a tenderness of father to son. His companion reached as well, to ape the familiarity of the king, but a shrill voice stopped him.

"Edward! Mon fil!' Isabella called from across the courtyard. She was unwilling to move closer, but insisted on his return to her.

"Your mother calls," Caernarfon said, with a sad plaint in his voice. He did not want it to be so, but since the death of his beloved friend Gaveston, whom Despenser replaced, the separation between them had been the only way he could keep peace among his house.

Edward reluctantly turned away and returned to his mother, feeling the chasm between his parents with every step.

The ceremonies were interrupted by the object of their exercise. A hale alarm was raised by the river wall and all turned attention to the Traitors Gate, which was opened to allow entrance from the river stream by a boat. Aboard the shallow-framed craft was a small company of three guards at arms, with a singular prisoner, bound and seated in the midst of them.

Edward strained to see the prisoner of whom he had heard much heated talk, but had never seen in the flesh himself. He had listened when he could to the arguments of his father's advisors of the Lord of Wigmore and the prowess of the knight of black unicorns. Would he be the monster of giant stature with an ogre's evil eye painted by his father's ministers' discussions?

As the boat bumped against the dock, steps down from the ground level of the castle courtyard, the guards arose from their seats and helped the condemned prisoner to rise in his manacles. Roger de Mortimer steadied his footing on the stone steps and walked, surrounded by the guards, toward the gaoler's apartments where he would be held until his appointed hour of death.

Edward's mother pulled her son back a few paces to allow the prisoner and his guards to pass. Edward studied the face of the traitor with curiosity, as if he might learn how to identify the breed, should he meet more in his time. Mortimer carried himself with a proud bearing, hardly the feted, fire-breathing creature of evil he expected. Edward was surprised that he thought him to have, in truth, a noble air of self-assurance. He did not notice that his mother was watching as intently as he, but with a different emotion.

All the company watched as Mortimer was led up the prison ward tower steps to the cells, until the doors slammed closed with a heavy rasp of locks.

4

The form of a man swam naked in the Thames where it flowed into the marshy thickets just downstream from the ramshackle wooden jumble of London, now spread beyond the city walls. The four rising corners of the White Tower of the castle guarding the river to the capital city were just visible above the trees. A clutch of retainers and ministers, impatient with papers to be signed, waited on the river bank with servants holding the king's robe and towel. Despenser stood closest to the shore, waiting as well, his feet sinking in the unsteady mud.

Caernarfon swam in leisurely strokes against the current. While still strong, it was slower here where the shallow marshes caught the tide, and the brown blobs of excrement caught among the reeds. Caernarfon enjoyed his swims, one of the few remaining athletics left of his youth. It was his respite from the demands which waited upon on shore. The putrid aroma of the city river was not his ideal pleasure, and far from the pristine nature of his country estates, but servants could wade ahead to catch and divert the blobbing waste which washed into the stream from the sewer sluices.

"Beware the turds, my lord," Despenser shouted in warning from the shore, with some amusement that the king insisted on taking his morning exercise in what water he could find.

The swimming king returned to the banks against the strong current. Despenser stepped further into the water to the calves of his purple stockings to help his friend and benefactor from the river. The body servants rushed forward with towels, but Despenser took a cloth from them to wipe down the king's glistening wet body himself. The lord ministers were careful to make no remark.

"A warning for life itself, mon petit," said Caernarfon. "Beware the turds. I prefer the fresher waters of our woods of Knaresborough, but the effluent of London is a distasteful necessity, if I am to keep my strength."

He now allowed his pages to dress him. The anxious ministers pressed forward with their parchments, but he waved them away, preferring to walk with Despenser. The ministers hung back, frustrated, whispering among themselves at the king and his confident, who spoke in hushed tones in French, so that they might not understand.

"A judgment of death lies on your enemy Mortimer by our efforts," Despenser said with satisfaction, "But your queen is—"

Caernarfon didn't let him finish the thought, reacting with a shiver, though whether from the dampness of his recent swim or the subject, was hard to distinguish. "Why does she hate me so? Have I not done my duty? I have adventured into that smelly sacred chalice and gifted her of four breathing offspring. I write her poems and she spits." It was a familiar complaint, but he could not help but add. "At least I'm sure three of my children are mine own issue."

"I delight in your poems, my lord," his favorite advisor offered in nearly sincere sycophancy.

Caernarfon touched his friend's face, teasing his thin beard with slender fingers. "A countenance worthy of verse." The king felt alone and the closeness of his confidante gave him comfort, but he noticed the ministers lagging behind and drew his hand away.

"Look at them," he said with disdain at the ever present retinue, who blamed him for so much, yet still demanded his largess, "the prunes."

It might be said that the king, this king, hated his position as much as he reveled in it.

"Taxes and tithes. Why should they care about my judgement?" he complained. "They grouse that the Bruce of Scotsland bested me at Bannockburn. Fifty-thousand English dead and they lay that at my feet!"

It was Scotland that remained a thorn in the paw of the English lion.

"Am I my father? Am I Longshanks?" he lamented, damning his own station. "He could pull apart Wallace and feast on his entrails. I prefer more delicate sweetbreads. He could ring the druids of heathen Wales with stone and iron, but I confess, war is a mystery to me. And it was Lancaster who withheld his full due of arms. Is that my blame?"

This was the principal issue which had brought them all to this moment. His cousin Lancaster had refused to deliver promised men-at-arms to the battle, and had stood against the king's granting of favor and properties on his unworthy confidante. The lords of the Welsh borderlands joined with the Lancasters against the king, from which three years of trials and blood had flowed.

Despenser now caressed his lord's face in tender comfort, "We will have our revenge upon them, my sweet Sire."

5

Edward sat on a stone parapet where he could see the river flowing below, as the sun sank into a cloying mist over the banks opposite where the slaughter house district of Londontown was set apart from the city. He was cutting at a long stick of wood, carving a sword. He surely had his ceremonial armor, fit to his size and fine steel sword as a prince of the realm, but was not allowed to carry a weapon on his person at court.

As he shaped the straight shard of Elder wood into the angular sides of a blade, it was King Arthur's Excalibur that was in his mind. He knew that he would not need to draw a sword from a stone to become king but often thought of how the great ancient king of glorious legends rose from a boy to a gracious, good, and wise leader of his people, and hoped he, too, might be so when he would be anointed.

The sound of a rattle of locks startled him as the great heavy door of the cell ward was thrust open, slamming against the stone, and a Kingsguard goaler shoved Roger Mortimer through the doorway. His ankles and wrists were manacled with chains, yet he was expected to take exercise, thus bound.

Both guard and prisoner were surprised to find the young prince on the battlement walk. The guard placed himself between his charge and the boy.

"This is not a fit place for you, Highness," he said with an uncertain authority.

Edward hopped off his stone perch. He was not of a mind to leave, fascinated by the chained lord, but not wanting to interfere with the guard's duty. He turned as if to go, but a rattling of the chains held him.

"You need have no dread of me, young prince," Mortimer spoke. His voice was deep and resonated with a melodic timber. Edward turned back to face him, for why should he be afraid of a condemned in chains. The two looked upon one another for what seemed an age passing.

"I am lunch," Mortimer said with a wry smile of a dark amusement, holding up his chained hands, aware of his fate. "I am the King's meat."

Edward drew himself up to as much height and dignity as he could present. "I do not fear of you, Sir. And if justice is true, you will not be my meal unless you deserve it."

Mortimer smiled. "Spoken like a king." He noticed the wood in Edward's hand. "What do you carve there? A sword? Learn to swing it well. It may serve you one day."

"If I honor valor and faith," Edward answered.

This made Mortimer smile again. He had heard that the king's eldest son fancied mythical tales of the days of old. "Then, you would be a chivalrous knight?"

"As those who sat at Arthur's table," the boy answered.

"The table round? At which all might be equal?" Mortimer knew the stories well himself. "Have you a favorite then, young prince? It is Lancelot? For his strength? Or Galahad, for his purity?"

"As one day I may sit at Arthur's place, I can have no favorites above the others, Sir."

Mortimer nodded, remarking that this regal heir would take equanimity as the object theme of the old stories, and not another. He would note this about the boy, as it might be useful should he survive.

"A lesson would only your father had learned," he said aloud.

"By what offense are you condemned?" Edward knew the general charge of treason but wanted to take the prisoner's measure.

"Fear," said Mortimer. "It is fear of me that offends your father's ministers. The lords of the western lands follow me."

"You are of the Marcher border? A Welsh man?" Edward thought much about the geography of the domains, for it was his birthright and his future to know them and the loyalties of those who held them, and to win them to him.

"Make no mistake. Though my lands lie in Wales and Ireland, I am of as noble Norman blood as your family. Save for my Spanish mother, from whom I inherited the discoloring of my eye." Mortimer paused for effect, pulling at the lower lid of his darker eye with his manacled hand.

Edward recoiled a moment, in a shiver of surprise, but then warmed by Mortimer's theatrical acceptance of this minor defect.

"Was it not from the misty glens of Carmarthen that Arthur and Merlin rose to unite the disaffected kingdoms?" Mortimer added.

"My father was Prince of Wales, named by my grandfather, born at Caernarfon."

Mortimer nodded. "I know this well. Your grandfather promised a son who would speak the ancient Briton lilt of the Welsh. But your father instead prefers the Normandy tongue of our forebears. And yet—" he paused, as if he might not say what was clearly on his mind.

The boy's curiosity was aroused by this. He wanted to understand. "You may speak plainly to me, sir. You are already condemned. I will not add to the charge if you confide to me."

Mortimer stated the cause. "Plainly, then. Your father relishes in his French origins and puts his trust in falsely influenced and unworthy friends."

"You blame his friends and say unworthy? What is unworthy in friendship?" Edward asked.

Mortimer considered his answer to the son of the king and how to state his case without making an enemy of the boy. "A man may have friends, but your father chooses his among the grasping and the unholy. Now, only the latest of preening peacocks."

Edward had heard the pejorative before. His mother often raged against the peacocks when she refused to let him visit his father. He didn't like it but intended to reason rather than insult. "My father's friends are my father's business. I should hope to have a free choice in my friends. You, sir, I might call a friend, at least for the short time before you lose a head."

Mortimer smiled at the riposte. A fair duel, he thought.

"My father has land holdings in France, and they will come to me," Edward reasoned. "My mother is of that country, and she believes we might be joined one day under my crown," Edward reasoned. "Should we not keep a close relation?"

"Your father's relations and your mother's are entirely separate issues." Mortimer said it with a certain weight which bothered Edward, but before he could ask what was meant, a door at the opposite end of the battlement walk rattled and opened.

Edward turned at the sound to see his mother, the queen, step from the royal apartments onto the defensive wall, just steps from the prison cells. She paused in the sunset breeze and looked to Mortimer with the guard and her son. She hesitated there.

The guard returned to his duty and shoved Mortimer back toward the stairs to his cell.

6

The guard outside the heavy, locked door of the prisoner's apartment sipped from a bowl of thin gruel. His lunch was small satisfaction for the long hours of standing. He was certain the condemned prisoner ate better than he, but satisfied himself that it was better than marching out in the cold breeze. He was startled by the rattle of keys on a belt and the glimmer of a candle at the end of the stone corridor.

A Warder led a lady in a dark cloak toward him, seen only by the flickering light of a burning taper. In her slender hands, she carried a plate covered by a cloth. He wondered if the kitchens were supplying the traitor with a second meal in expectation of his soon arriving end, but when the lady's face was glimpsed beyond the edge of the cloak hood, the revelation made him forget his appetite entirely. He dropped to a knee, to bow his head.

"Your Majestic Grace," he uttered.

It was the queen, Isabella, who carried the platter. She smiled at the lowly guard and pulled the cloth away to reveal a pile of food, as if left from a banquet. There was mutton and bread, and some figs.

"Sir, I worry for your health in this dark space," Isabella smiled, flirting with him. "And such meager sustenance to protect us from a dangerous prisoner."

The Warder took the plate from her hands and set it beside the guard's station. The guard could think of nothing worthy he might say, trying not to stare at the face he had only until now seen in paint and on coins, and bowed his thanks.

Mortimer paced in his apartment cell, a bed and writing table the only furnishings. His thoughts were of how his life had been reduced to such a small confine. He, who had won victories on the fields and served at the hands of kings, whose place should have been his, was now only to count the several hours, in the amount of flagstones in the floor. He could now hear the voices outside the chamber door, and soon keys rattled in the lock.

The door was thrown open by the Warder, and Isabella hurried into the room. She did not wait for privacy, but rushed to Mortimer's arms. They kissed as the Warder discreetly withdrew from the chamber, closing the door and leaving the candle.

Mortimer tasted her kiss and held her face. "If every man's last supper could taste as sweet, how many more would seek the headsman's ax?"

Isabella melted into him, feeling his heavy arms. He was near old enough to be her father, and perhaps even was the shadow of the father she wished hers was. The strength in those arms was indeed more comforting, even in a prison cell, than the weak meal of her arranged and now reviled husband.

"Do not joke with me," she chided. "There is little time. Your guard quickly fills his hunger." She handed him folded parchments, returning her intention to the business of his rescue.

"You have made the arrangements, then?" His hope rose. He had not been certain he had won her fully, but here she was.

"A boatman waits at the river to carry you to Calais. These will give you safe passage to my newly crowned brother's court. Phillip will be our ally."

Mortimer held her cheeks in his hands, hoping to seal the bargain with the payment she craved. "Can I part from this face, worthy of a thousand ships, for only one small boat?"

Isabella rejoiced in his clever compliments. "Flattery earns you a kiss, my lord. Loyalty may earn a kingdom." She kissed him once again, assuring him, "I will follow soon. The king dares not leave these shores with such an unhappy mood among the people. He sends our son to kneel for his lands in Aquitaine."

"Then I'll save my best jokes for a return to England and tell them to your husband."

Mortimer emerged from the cell behind Isabella. The corridor was silent, the Warder gone. Their feet stepped over the lump of the guard, lying still on the stones, in a pool of vomited poisoned victuals. Isabella hurried back toward the royal apartments, while her lover went opposite, carrying the dagger she had given him for his protection.

Another unlucky soldier stood lonely guard by the boat dock that night. Mortimer appeared from the shadows and thrust a dagger into his ribs. He held the heavy body briefly before allowing the dead man to slip into the mucky Thames as a small boat rowed up to the dock from the river shoal.

A watchman called out "All is Well!" somewhere from the battlements above as the oarsman rowed the boat with the prisoner into the foggy shadows of the night.

~~~

CHAPTER THREE

1

12th Day of October, 1326

Low sea cliffs rose above the wide beach to green fields above on the plain of Calais. There, tents of a gathered army of a bare few hundred men-at-arms and scarce knights prepared for an impending campaign in the misty distance, where steeper cliffs of white chalk waited.

A Peregrine falcon soared through the crisp, cloudless air. It swooped and gamboled on the gusty coastal breezes, as if free from earthly bonds. Suddenly, the powerful bird tumbled from its path and struck a fleeting dove, snatching the prey in its talons. The predator carried its prize a short distance before unnaturally releasing it to fall to the grassy field as a leather gloved hand extended into the air. The falcon swooped to latch onto it, tearing at a piece of raw meat held in the crux of the thumb and forefinger.

The glove was Mortimer's. It had been near two years since his escape from the cell of the Tower. His time in France had served him well. He was refreshed and restored in good health, and had made good friends in the French court as well as communications with friends to the north, who felt as injured by the English king as he. Isabella and Edward had joined him scarce three months on, and they had been constant companions.

Edward had taken Mortimer as a friend to his mother, while he had learned the ways of his class in the foreign court.

"You prefer the Peregrine to the Ger, Lord Mortimer?" he asked, as they rode three together on the Calais cliff, within short sight of the armed camp.

"Oh, the Peregrine from the crags of Carmarthen is far superior to the English bird," Mortimer offered as the animal fluttered its wings.

"But why do you fly the female bird?"

"In her species, the lady is swifter and more powerful than the male. But she needs special care." Mortimer took a swig of water from his pouch skin and sprayed it from his mouth in droplets. The bird preened, enjoying the cooling bath.

Mortimer and Isabella's eyes met past the boy as Mortimer took a piece of raw meat between his lips and allowed the bird to snatch the snack with its beak, a dangerous kiss.

Edward was impressed with Mortimer's assured confidence. It could be said he was as seduced in affection as his mother.

A hunting horn sounded from below, where a meal had been laid out near their tent on the beach.

"I'll race you to lunch, my lord," Edward challenged, but did not wait for the response, eagerly spurring his horse and galloping away.

"Be careful!" Isabella shouted after her son, as she always worried for his exuberance, then smiled at her Mortimer, "It is good you win him to you."

Mortimer nodded with a knowing smile, for he too was pleased, and spurred his horse, chasing after Edward.

Mortimer stood over the table where the finished roast chicken and figs had been pushed aside to make room for a map of England. Isabella sat beside him, going over the map. Edward watched them from the opposite side, in the shade of the flapping tent. He was glad to see his mother intent on her plans, and seemingly content, as she discussed strategies with the noble soldier. It was an image of closeness he had seen in others' parents, but could not recall the same of his own. He stepped around to join his mother when Mortimer was distracted for a moment.

"Are you happy, Maman? You were unhappy for so long."

Isabella touched her son as a mother might, warmed by his concern. "Mortimer's friendship makes Isabel smile. He is a true ally in her eyes," she said, referring to herself, as she often did, as if she was a separate person, two lives lived together in parallel.

"Then, I am happy," Edward said, and meant it.

Their attention was caught by four men riding leisurely up the beach toward the tent. At the lead was Henry, Earl of Lancaster, having gained the title after his elder brother had perished in the attack upon the road. At two years of sixty in age, he was a once powerful knight bending under time's thumb. His was a rather unkempt appearance for a great nobleman, a scraggly beard, and unwashed clothes worn too many days to save on the expense when he could easily afford it, and carried himself with an overly stiff bearing as if always in pain. He was also prone to flatulence.

With him rode young noble knights who were among the cadre who had defended Lancaster on the road against the king's men.

Lord William Montagu, a dashingly intense looking young man of four and twenty, Sir John Beaumont and Sir Robert Holland, who were among the barons who had defended Lancaster.

Isabella stood from her cushioned stool. "Welcome, cousin Lancaster."

"Do not rise on my account, Cousin. Queens may go before Earls," Lancaster spoke from his saddle.

Isabella held her tone. "Except as your English Parliament would have it." It was an old wound. She had pressed her case against her husband before that body of barons but had been spurned by the majority, too many unwilling to take the side of one of her sex against the even less-than-valiant monarch.

"Milady takes too much notice of our heated arguments. It is politics." Lancaster dismounted his horse with full throated fart, an added note to his diplomacy.

Edward exchanged a disgusted glance with Mortimer as the old man glanced over the lunch table with the map.

"Brisk and fervent parlay is our sustenance." The old baron continued with a dark gallows wit. "The commoners, in particular, have an appetite for feasting on their betters."

The old earl ruffled young Edward's hair, annoying him greatly. "And how fairs my princely nephew?" Without waiting for answer, he introduced the others.

"May I present William, Lord de Montagu, you know, I believe, and Sirs Beaumont and Holland, who may be new to your ken."

Beaumont bowed to the queen, but Holland eagerly took to a knee in the wet sand at the lady's feet and took her hand to kiss her ring. "Your Grace, thy beauty outshines the legends! I swear my life to your cause against the king who so mistreats your honor."

Isabella beamed at the flattery. "You honor me greatly with your pledge, good sir."

"Shall we to the business, then?" Lancaster felt the tick of time's clock and had little to spare for flattery. "I am told Your Grace has raised a force of three thousand from your Flemish cousin to move against your husband."

Isabella nodded the truth of it while Lancaster helped himself to a chicken leg from the lunch table spread, gnawing as he spoke, with bits of grease and skin in his beard, as unkempt as a bird's nest.

"And will the French king lend his support?" he asked.

"I have pleaded with him, but he is afraid of war," she answered honestly, but held back her fury at her cousin, who had refused her.

In spite of her claims of betrayed honor and argument that France might press advantage on England, the young king Phillip's advisors resisted. They countered that her father had supported Scottish claims in war on the northern borders of the neighbor kingdom, but while victory had been gained in battle, stalemate was the result at a heavy cost. The French king was new on the throne and the people not soon disposed to taxation for more adventures on foreign lands.

Isabella had not made the case in open of her belief the French crown should have passed to her upon her father's death, rather than Phillip, who was not of his direct blood but born of their mother's line.

She had resolved that this was a cause she would make once she had secured the English crown. But she revealed none of this thought to the lord ally she needed who stood before her disgustingly feasting himself on her left-overs.

Lancaster considered as he chewed, "Then, at least he will stay neutral."

Edward whispered to his mother with derision, "He has ill manners, this old fart! He disgraces chivalry."

Isabella quieted him with an amused 'shush', agreeing with him.

Lancaster tossed the bone and licked his fingers. "No man hungers more to be returned to his lands than I, but I question what form of governing my Lady Cousin envisions should we prevail?"

"I will see my husband removed and his son made king."

"Surely you intend no violence against your husband's person. Would it not cause less upheaval if Caernarfon were left as king—guided, of course, by our Parliament, as was the intent of the Great Charter? Which I hope we all serve."

Lancaster cast a glance to Mortimer, who had been silent. Although they had found themselves on the same side of an issue against the king, there was little love between these two powerful men, and even less trust.

"And give greater power to the barons?" Isabella snapped, allowing her anger to surface. "No. The king must go."

Mortimer spoke as if he might close the case. "If it ease your mind, Lancaster, I stand with our Queen. And many stand with me. We will have a new king."

Mortimer clapped his hand on the young prince's shoulder and Edward stood a little taller. He felt pride that he was the object of this fight. He had made himself familiar with the case of his mother against his father, whom he had come in his time away to feel as if forsaken by him. It was Mortimer who had been as a father to him in the absence of blood family.

"It eases me little, my Lord Mortimer," Lancaster quipped as he looked from Isabella to the older ambitious lord beside her. "How fairs your wife in your absence? Well, I hope."

"Well."

"And your children?"

"Well."

It was open to anyone who might have eyes that Mortimer had left his wife in charge of his lands and estates while he remained at the side of Isabella, forsaking hearth and home for her bed while in exile in France. Edward studied the old man for his mood, even though he did not like his manner. He believed his education was as much to understand what his friends and his enemies might truly think and mean, though they may not speak their intent.

Lancaster at last made a rueful smile.

"Well, then, it appears I am outnumbered. What say you, Montagu?" he turned to the younger. "You know the minds of the lesser Lords."

Montagu did not speak for a moment, staring at Edward, sizing him up. He was an intense looking young man of four and twenty years. His father had fought beside Longshanks and he had himself gained glory in the Scottish battles, and been granted a baronetcy by the second Edward, but had grown as discontent as any among them. He had accompanied Isabella and the prince on their mission to the French court as royal guard, and had conversations with the boy, whom he found agile of mind and eager to fulfill duty.

"A healthy meal requires a fresh fish," was Montagu's reply, with a small smile as he did enjoy his own wit. "I'll stand for a new king, if he be just."

"If I am to be a king, I vow I shall be the greatest ever in fairness of spirit, and bring honor to the codes of chivalry," proclaimed young Edward, for he did believe it.

The adults surrounding him smiled at youth's enthusiasm, for they all professed the code he took to heart, but knew well the difficulty in practice.

Lancaster bowed to Isabella, "It seems then, your will takes the day, my majestic cousin." He pointed with a bony finger, made crooked by the ague of the joints, to the map spread before them. "But we may only hope it is God's will that we take the hard days ahead. The king's brother, of Kent, awaits us at Dover. He has at last fallen to our side."

"You do bring good news, then." Isabella brightened with the knowledge that with the king's brother on their side, they could not be repelled at the shore and their cause was ever more hopeful. He had been the last to defend his brother and his rightful hold on the crown. He was no friend to Isabella, but she knew he was fond of her son. She would use this.

Edward beamed happily. "My uncle joins us? It has been so long since I have seen him, Maman." Edward had fond memories of his uncle, who was most alike in temperament to himself in his family.

"You will see him soon, then lad," Lancaster announced, expanding to his full height as if years might fall away like the crust of old battle iron left to rust is shed with oil in preparation for a new contest. "Before the tide has changed, we will take sword to the shores of home."

"Hail, Isabella! For England!" shouted the young barons and knights, eager for glory.

So, for the coast of chalk they sailed. A small force of two thousand men to follow the queen's banner. Fifty ships provided from the land of the Hainaut and the queen's own French county of Ponthieu sailed against the currents of the sea in a blustery gale, toward the Dover cliffs, where they were greeted by a happy throng. The people lined the crumbling edge to look where the sails of William and the first Normans had appeared near two-hundred and fifty years before.

The queen's party of knights rode from the vessels moored below the chalk cliffs, toward the high perched castle of the king's brother. At the head were old Lancaster and Montagu, with Mortimer just behind, and others of the company. The townsfolk lined the road to catch a glimpse of the queen's beauty of legend and song, and were surprised as she rode a horse as well, not carried by servant slaves like Cleopatra, but upright and proud, as if a warrior queen, to save them. Beside her rode the handsome boy they knew as Windsor, who might be king, and behind him his brother, John and young sister Joan, both fine examples of their family, and they cheered, for at that moment, it was good to be English.

When the column approached the chasm before the castle walls, the drawbridge lowered on clanking chains in welcome. As the beams thudded on their stops, revealed standing alone in the midst of the arch entrance beyond was the roguishly cheerful face of Edmund, Earl of Kent, the brother who had near slit the throat of the Valois now King of France over the christening of the Prince of Wales. Edmund was approaching his fortieth year but as full of youthful cheer as his early days, his blue eyes crinkled at the edge above his blond beard, trimmed close. Drink and pleasure had made his former sharp cheekbones just a bit puffy in flesh.

At the sight of his uncle, Edward jumped from his horse and ran to meet him at the middle of the draw span, his boy's sword wagging at his belt.

"Uncle Edmund!" he cried in joy.

Edmund caught the excited boy in his arms and swirled him around, then set him down with a hearty slap on the shoulder.

"Why, you've grown like a thistle! I do swear it! Wait! What's this?" He reached behind Edward's ear and pulled out a coin with his brother's face upon it. "Still saving your pennies?"

"Do another, Uncle!" Edward laughed.

Yet, Edmund turned to a serious tone. "No, the season for boyish tricks is past. You are soon to be a man, Edward. It is time you learned a man's art." He suddenly grasped the small ceremonial sword from Edward's scabbard and held it derisively. "A weapon not fit for a whipping boy, alone, a Prince!" And he tossed it over the side of the drawbridge, tumbling into the chasm. Then he drew his own long sword, offering it. Edward was hardly able to lift the heavy weapon, forged of sharp steel. Edmund easily dodged his playful thrusts, parrying with a gloved hand.

"Never worry, you will grow larger than the sword,' Edmund laughed heartily, then greeted his approaching allies. "Cousin Lancaster! And Wigmore. Welcome." Though, his greeting of Mortimer held a reserve and a cautious air.

"What's the news of your brother's forces?" Lancaster asked with expectation.

And the news, Edmund was glad to give. "Word of your coming has spread and the people have taken up the cry. My brother has lost allies in the north and holds strong only in the west. He headquarters at Kenilworth and guards the Thames and the Avon.

"Then we must waste no time," said Mortimer, hungry for battle.

"Time is only wasted in haste," Edmund answered. "Let me get to know my nephew before we steal his youth."

Edmund knew Mortimer from the battlefield. And he knew his ambitions. What he did not know was what had been the effect on his young nephew's mind, all this time in his care, and among the distrusted French.

Edmund and Edward walked along the chalky cliffs with kestrels soaring above while the growing army was supplied from the shallow draft ships on the beach.

"How did you entertain yourself among our cousins, young wart?" Edmund asked in the jest of an uncle, though his purpose was as sharp as a needle. "Did you develop an appetite for frogs? A nose for the scent of crushed weeds?"

Edward had heard the story of his birth, and his uncle's near bringing two countries to war over his name. He knew that Edmund could not set foot as an Englishman in France and was wary of returning the favor. There were a contingent of Flemish knights in the forces of the queen from her Valois cousin in Hainaut who held allegiance to the crown of France and archers from Aquitaine, who swore to the English crown but lived their lives as Frenchmen.

"The young ladies of court were darker and sharper than I have seen before," said Edward, allowing himself to share what he could not with his close cadre of retainers, employed by his mother, who might pass secrets, but now free to share with a like spirit.

Edmund smiled, for he understood. "You take notice of ladies, then. You have grown since last we spoke. You may soon discover the pleasure is in the sampling from the tray."

Edward blushed, for he had come of age while in France, with nocturnal explosions, first sudden and fierce. Then, everywhere he looked, shapes of girls' bodies he could glimpse in folds of linen and damask had drawn his attention as they had not before. A handsome young prince in a foreign court, who would attract the eyes and whispers of nearly any young lady he might pass.

Edmund smiled with knowing, chiding him to confess, "You have tasted a flavor, then?"

"I swear I did not."

"Lie to your mother, not thy uncle. Your secret is safe."

There was a moment, briefly behind a tapestry, where Edward had found a young waiting-maid who placed his hands among the folds of her shift and allowed him to smell the most extraordinary aroma of her wetness on his fingers before she attempted to do something with her hand but ended with such a swift resolution he could scarcely believe it was not a dream, nor ask her name before she ran away.

"I swear," he said again.

Edmund accepted his plead of chastity, whether from embarrassment or chivalry. "And your French cousin, new on his throne? What was your opinion when you scraped your knee and bowed your head?"

"The former king was called Fair, but he seemed to me weak and pale, this Phillip. And my mother was angry with you, Uncle, for your delay in joining us."

Edmund signaled him to draw close in confidence, a whispered confession of his true feeling, even though no-one was close enough to hear. "If it were the azure and lilies of France unloading arms below, rather than Hainaut, my greeting would be steel and blood. I did not save you from an unfortunate name to hand our land to the family Valois in place of my brother."

"Would you not take my father's place if the country willed it?" Edward asked.

"I would not take his chair for the world," was Edmund's reply. "For he carries the burden of our father's reputation, and that is a heavy load for which I care not. A goblet of wine, or a sword, suits my hand better than a scepter."

"What is your opinion of my father?" Edward asked. He had heard many opinions, from those who hated him and those who did not know him in person.

Edmund was in neither of those categories, and he answered with a weight of sadness. "He gives his heart too freely to those who would flatter him. So, now he has armies arrayed against him.'

He braced Edward on the shoulder, sensing his conflicted feelings. "I do not blame him for whom he chooses to love. I do blame your mother for not letting you know him better."

And then he offered a simple and sincere warning. "Beware nephew, of those who would draw advantage from your friendship. For it is those nearest who may offer sustenance to your pride, yet may not be your true friends."

~~~

CHAPTER FOUR

1

14th Day of January, 1327

For three months, young Edward traveled with his mother's army, learning the ways of battle at the side of powerful Mortimer, Lancaster, and his uncle. Montagu and Holland were given the honor of his personal protection, and they became friends. As more joined them, the king's forces collapsed and what remained crossed the River Severn. They made for the Despenser lands of Wales, hoping to reach the strong iron ring fortresses of Caernarfon's father still loyal to him. The final battle came in the southern lands of Glamorgan, at the castle called Nedd, where Caernarfon and his favorite were besieged.

As the army rode from the trees toward the castle, the heavy drawbridge was raised on its clanking chains. Swords clashed as Isabella's knights fought the remaining soldiers of the king's guard from their mounts on the bridge of the castle. Mortimer fought mightily with Edmund beside him as arrows rained down from the parapets, striking the knights around them, many arrows glancing from the plate, while others struck home through mail and leather.

Edward observed the fierce battle from a safe vantage beyond the bridge with awe, and his mother beside him, triumphant as she knew her cause was nearing a victory.

"But how will they breach the draw?" he wondered, as at last the only remaining boundary was the span of the canal and gate.

"Watch," was her answer.

Mortimer and Edmund together broke through the guards and rode to the chasm before the raised drawbridge. Edmund dropped from his horse, while Mortimer signaled to the nearby woods. Pikemen dashed forward to the edge of the moat, launching their pikes like spears, which embedded deeply into the wood of the raised bridge.

Edmund dashed and leaped across the chasm to the pikes. While defenders fired arrows from the murder holes but too narrow an angle to reach him, the brave earl climbed the pike lances like a ladder to the top of the drawbridge. He swung his sword down on the rope of the counterweight and rode the heavy bridge as it fell to the stops with a thunderous crack.

Sappers rolled barrels of tar across the bridge to slam against the wooden gate, the last obstacle to entry. Archers fired flaming arrows to alight the tar to burn. The blaze of fire consumed the gate and the screams of defenders trapped inside the gate house defenses drifted across the moat ditch. When the fire had done its work, the siege ram broke through the still flaming charred beams.

Mortimer charged his horse across the bridge at the head of the other knights into the castle, through damaged gates, followed by Edmund and the rest of the Queen's Men.

The castle chambers were ill defended as if the cause was hopeless and few of the king's remaining servants had the will to serve to the death, and so surrendered. A search was made to find the king and his hated exchequer. The search at last found them together in the king's apartment.

Edward Caernarfon and Despenser were found in bed together, a dagger between them. They had intended suicide but delayed in their purpose as the inner door burst open. The men of the queen's arms rushed in, in time to stop them. Mortimer entered the chamber with Isabella, followed by Lancaster and lastly with him, Edward. The young prince could only stare bewildered at the sight of his father in bed, dressed in only a bare shift, with another man.

"Father?" was all the boy could utter before Mortimer stepped toward the bed, drawing his sword. The king drew up, prepared for death, but Lancaster interceded between them.

"Edward of Caernarfon, fear not for your life." Lancaster spoke as he believed he had agreed with the queen was their purpose, fixing his gaze on the man beside him. "Our quarrel is with those you have placed above your subjects and your duty. We, the Barons of England, by rights of the Magna Carta hereby revoke your honor of Kingship and name your son, Edward, of Windsor, in your place until such time as he may be duly crowned at Westminster."

Yet, his charge could not hold back Mortimer's enmity at his principal enemy. He advanced on the younger Despenser with his bloodied sword blade. "As for this dog who has usurped the Queen's rightful place—!"

Despenser crawled from the bed feathers to Isabella, kneeling in front of her with his hands folded, pleading for her mercy in French. "Ma tres belle Dame Majestie! Ayez pitie de moi! Pardon—"

"I yet smile, Monsieur." Mortimer grinned in twisted revenge, "For my lady's honor!" With a vicious swiftness, Mortimer brought his sword down onto the kneeling figure with force near enough to split him, the blade only stopped by thick, resistant cartilage. Edward flinched as he was splattered with his father's lover's blood.

The human form can endure many wounds for a time. Despenser was not killed outright but lingered in pain to stand at a swift public trial where Mortimer and Isabella were heartily cheered by the happy throngs who believed they were their saviors from tyranny's yoke. The king's favorite was sentenced to be drawn and quartered. The first blow was struck by Isabella herself, castrating him before the crowd, holding the "jewels" aloft in her bloody hand for her revenge and symbol of the end of his issue.

The executioners performed their work of slitting him open while alive to draw out his entrails, and as his life expired, butchered his body into four sections, with the head removed to be placed upon a spike on the London bridge in sight of the Westminster palace.

Caernarfon was not forced to witness the execution, but had been removed to Lancaster's care and protection at the fortress of Kenilworth.

2

The castle of Kenilworth had been one of the strongest fortresses in the midlands since the days of the conquest. King John had added outer walls and a double moat when he made it into one of his palaces. It had withstood a year long siege, even assault by barge in a rebellion of Henry of Hastings. It was now under the charge of Henry of Lancaster, one of the lands restored to him that had been taken by the Despensers upon the death of his brother.

The walls of the armory were lined with the tools of war, swords, pikes, and lances arranged in neat ranks. Isabella and Mortimer stood impatiently over an anguished young Edward. Close by them were

Lancaster, Edmund, and a cruel-looking man in rich cleric's robes, Adam of Orleton, the Bishop of Hereford, an ally to Isabella and Mortimer.

The young prince was unhappy. The king was held only just above them within the castle, but Edward was kept from him. "Why won't you let me see my father?!" he pleaded. "He cannot be the monster you say!"

"You are too young to understand his evil. You will not see or speak to him while I have breath," Isabella spoke with a pure certainty. Their purpose was for Edward to acquiesce to the decision which had been agreed by parliament, that he take the place of his father upon the throne. As heir, and the object of months of bloody war, he had not taken part in the arguments and was the last to accept this extraordinary redress of injury, never before done in this or any land before, where council of men would replace a Holy anointed king by act of democracy. But it was not politics which pulled at his heart.

Mortimer knelt beside him to speak soothingly, trying to distract his need. "Edward, I know you ache for a father. But now you must do as your mother and duty command. When you need a father's comfort, call upon me."

Slowly, a change seemed to well up from deep inside Edward and sweep over him like an inner wind. He drew himself up, wiping all traces of tears from his cheeks. He understood it was a mantel he must bear. He had trained for it since his youngest days.

"Then, I will do my duty. From this day I am no longer a boy, but a king."

Lancaster advanced, drawing his sword, "If you are to be King, you must first be knight. Kneel. There is no time for ceremony."

"May not Mortimer do it?" Edward asked.

"He is not of your station," was the sharp reply.

Disappointed, Edward dropped to one knee. He had long thought of this moment of his life. He had expected with great anticipation how it would feel to receive his knighthood, to turn from child to man. In other circumstance, the investiture would have taken a week of solemn preparation and celebration, but their cause was immediate and the old man he thought disgusting the one to do it.

Lancaster held the sword aloft, pronouncing the invocation of knighthood, and tapped him on the left shoulder, then the right. Edward kissed the point of the blade. Then he looked up to those around him.

"But I won't accept my father's title until he freely resigns it," he said with a will of his own. "It will not be said I am a son who cast down my own father because I wanted his crown."

Mortimer was taken by surprise by this unexpected demand. He coolly turned to Isabella, who seemed at a loss.

"What do we do?" she whispered.

"We must fulfill his wish," said Mortimer as the method came into his mind. He left Isabella to join in quiet conference with the Bishop Orleton, in whose direct charge the king was held.

"Orleton," Mortimer whispered aside, "go to the king's prison above and extract the resignation the boy requires, by whatever churchly means serve you best. We must have his agreement."

Orleton nodded understanding and stepped from the hall. Now risen to Bishop of Hereford, Orleton, who bore the given name of the first of man in the garden, Adam, had been a close confident of the Mortimers since his youth. He had served as counsel at the Papal court at Avignon of Clement V, and nominated for bishop by John XXII. It was in the tribunal judgments at the courts of inquisition where he learned the methods of extracting confessions and signatures upon sworn false testaments.

The chamber where the king was held had been made devoid of all former royal trappings, now only a cold stone room with a bed of straw and a table. Bishop Orleton stood aside while two burly knights assigned as jailers, Sir John Maltravers and Sir John Gourney, tightened a leather thong around Caernarfon's throat and thrust his head into a vat of icy water.

The king, now brought to his lowest estate, sank to his knees, his face anguished as the water dripped from his hair and the shrinking leather bit into his neck. He cried in despair, "If my son wishes this, why will he not visit me?" He did not know that Edward wanted to see him, but was being kept from him, made to think his son hated him.

Orleton stepped to the tub, and pulled up his Bishop's surcoat to piss into the water, to make it more shameful. The jailers thrust him in once again, holding his head in the water so that he might feel he would drown. This had proved most effective in encouraging the confession of witches, so they might more efficiently be put to the flame. Orleton held out a paper for Caernarfon to sign his mark.

3

1st Day of February, 1327

Bells rang from the tower of the Abbey of Westminster as the crown of St George, gleaming in light, was held aloft by the Archbishop of Canterbury. Edward, with the regal robe about his shoulders and sword girth at his waist, stepped to the dais. He paused as his uncle Edmund, at his side, bent close to whisper in his ear.

"Remember when you take your vow, Nephew, God lays his hand on you to be sovereign over your subjects, not for your benefit, but for your protection of their good."

Edward heard the words and nodded solemnly as Edmund stepped away for Edward to accept the anointment, lowering to his knees before the Archbishop in front of the coronation throne. The crown was lowered onto his head as the choir's song filled the arches of the abbey as if reaching to heaven. The bells rang throughout the town and heralds rode to shout the news of a newly crowned king.

"Long live the King! Hail, Edward! Long live the boy King!"

Yet, even as the coronation bells rang, and the crowds shouted joyously rejoicing, inside the walls of Westminster were gathered the most powerful lords of Parliament, deciding the issues to control their lives. Lancaster's lands taken by the Despensers were fully restored, making the northern earl the most powerful among them, and placed in charge of the new king's welfare and protection. The Queen Isabella had fully expected of those who had sworn faith to her cause that she would be set as Regent for her son, to make royal decisions in his stead until his majority, but she had been disappointed. Wary of such power in one hand, Parliament instead had decreed a Council of Regency, twelve appointed lords who together would make sovereign action. The queen was most distressed that she should be denied.

Lancaster interceded with the queen outside of the chamber hall to gain her acquiescence and keep peace.

"I do not understand this Council of Regency! It has always been for one regent to be vested until the king reaches maturity and that should be his mother!" she argued with her fury only contained enough that her words might not be heard inside the voting hall.

"My Lady Cousin," said Lancaster, "with all due respect for Your Grace, and your gentle sex, this country has just been delivered from one set of over-reaching governors. We have no stomach to trade for another."

Isabella fumed, "You are calling me unfit? Comparing me to those creatures!" She referred to the list of the twelve lords who had been chosen by the full Parliament to sit on the council, many of them who had taken her husband's cause against her.

"No, Cousin, we only say our best protection against further civil strife is this Council of Twelve. It is by this means we have brought together the two sides who see opposite faces of the coin and have brought our war to a common end." But Isabella had little patience for this diplomacy.

Mortimer stepped to the seething lady. "Look over the list again," he urged, whispering with a soothing voice in her ear. He had not gained the lands of

Lancaster, but his part and promises in the campaign which had brought down the king had given him a strong voice in the choosing of the council. "Of the twelve, you will count among them seven who may be called 'Mortimer's men'."

Isabella calmed her present ire, intending to negotiate her position. "Lord Mortimer urges me to take your proposal under advisement."

Lancaster presented her the parchment with the council decree and listed members, with no room for negotiation. "This is no proposal, my lady. We of Parliament, Lords and Commoners, have all signed it in several."

With a cool glance to Mortimer, she handed the paper back, taking no notice of the text.

"Then, I have no choice but to accept. Pardon." With a flourish, she gathered her skirts and glided to the door, throwing it open. The barons bowed to the queen. Mortimer followed her.

Isabella's fury carried her to the cloisters of the abbey, far enough that the lords gathered in the palace hall to rule over her could not hear her shout of fury. Mortimer caught her to soothe her.

"This pack of wolves!" she raged. "They howl because I am a woman who sups at men's table. Since this English Charter, they believe they may usurp the divinely bestowed royal power. God will strike down their pride!"

Mortimer knew her moods well, which, with the passing time between them had grown in tidal swing. He was more prepared for the long contest of move and counter than she. His long wait in captivity had given him room to plan for what obstacles might come before them. "This is a game not for God, Isabella, but for cunning. We will turn their pride to our advantage."

Yet, Isabella was gripped by another thought which more and more had taken root in her mind. "Or does their loyalty fail because I pass another year? Is this why they abandon me like my husband before?"

Even Mortimer was surprised by the suddenness of the turn of her thoughts. He reassuringly took her in his arms.

"Do not waste your passions on these lesser men, for I require all you possess." He took her openly in his arms among the cloisters and kissed her, so that she might forget politics. She was comforted in his grasp, allowing for the present moment the woman to take preeminence over queen, but their peace was only for a fleeting time.

A page messenger hurried through the filigreed arches, searching for them with a look of urgency, clutching a folded and sealed paper.

"Your Grace," he bowed to the queen, but quickly turned to Mortimer, offering the missive. Mortimer grasped it to open and read. Isabella watched his face, which by turns changed from concern to hope, as if the world might have shifted in a few lines.

"What is it?" Isabella asked, in curiosity at what could cause such a change.

"The Black Douglas has crossed the Roman Wall with a small force of raiders," he answered, with a secretive satisfaction.

"The Scots?" She was bewildered that a former ally against her husband might turn upon them so quickly. "King Robert is near his death. He can't want to start a war?" But she again looked at Mortimer's countenance to read his calm mood, as if it was no surprise. "Did you know of this? Did the Scottish ambassadors make mention of this while we were in France?"

Mortimer dismissed the messenger and waited for him to go from hearing before speaking of his private knowledge. "We had many discussions of where our common interests might meet," he said with a satisfaction, as if he knew more than he would say, even to her. "The Bruce is anxious to regain his borderlands before his soul departs this earth and his heart carried to the Holy Land. I suspect he wants to take the measure of our new boy king. He sends the Douglas to provoke our nerve."

"What is in your mind?" Isabella knew there was more. She was certain he had already considered a course.

Mortimer was clear in the path he saw laying out before them. "War requires the raising of money," he said, testing to reveal his thoughts to her by degrees. He needed her trust. "And money yields loyalties."

And even as the course became clearer in his mind, the obstacles before them seemed to meld into the one solution. "A war, too, would bring some distraction to your eager son. And if managed with care, balance this Council of Twelve more to our advantage." He reasoned out for her, joining two obstacles into one solution. "I know of two more northern lords who would add to our seven if war was made."

Isabella marveled at the clarity of his mind, reminded why she had been drawn to him and only made her love him more.

And so, even on the very day of the coronation of the fresh English boy king, Scots raiders struck at the town of Norham, across the River Tyne, south of the ruin of the great wall left by the Roman emperor Hadrian. The stones which had formed the great barrier against the wild northern clans had long since been stolen to make the streets and churches of

Northumberland, with nothing to protect the English from Scottish fury, save treaty and good will.

The raiders on horseback were led by a fierce, battle scarred knight in black armor over his clan kilt. James O'Douglas, whose own father had joined against the English crown and had died in the London Tower, had been made the First Lord of Scotland by his king, Robert Bruce, after the victory of Bannockburn, and who through skilled prowess in past battles had gained the fearful name of "The Black Douglas". The raiders galloped through the village streets tossing torches onto the thatched houses, setting the town ablaze as they shouted the names of the dead clan warriors of the past, Wallace and MacGregor, laid to grave by the first Edward.

4

A great army was raised and gathered at York. There were four thousand knights and nobles, ten thousand men-at-arms, and twenty thousand long-bow archers. The sounds of horses and soldiers clattered in the narrow cobblestone streets. The signs of war preparations showed everywhere. Food was prepared and packed, weapons sharpened, carts and wagons loaded. Soldiers lounged about, throwing dice, roughhousing, all of them to be led into battle by a young king wishing to prove himself.

Edward, king for not half a year and still a boy of fourteen, walked among the wagons with Mortimer and his Uncle Edmund flanking him, inspecting his troops. As the surprised soldiers realized who the boy was, they knelt dutifully as he passed. Edward was truly amazed by it all.

William, the Count of Hainaut, Zeeland and Holland, the queen mother's cousin by marriage to Joan of Valois, had brought three thousand men to aid in the campaign. He had also brought the ladies of his court, and young Edward's journey to manhood was to begin, it might be said, when he first saw the sun shine at night.

A celebration in advance of war was held in the great hall of the royal castle of York, within that northern city's great walls. Boar and pheasant turned on the spits. Lords and ladies danced and drank from the wassail. Minstrels strolled among them, singing songs of the glorious days of Roland and Arthur, while puppeteers performed pantomimes for the children. The battles to come for which they had gathered seemed far distant.

Isabella delighted in playing hostess, showing off her latest gown of Dutch velvets, brought by her cousin from the weaving mills of their great industry, accented by silks and jewels. It was a conspicuous display of growing wealth, which she believed to represent the prosperity of her country without the deposed king and his favorites, though while the people still rejoiced, many in court suspected they had just, again, traded one grasping favorite for another.

The boy king was among the dancers capering to the lute with a young noble girl. He danced with grace, while finding it difficult to keep the man-sized crown on his head, having to hold it with one hand when he turned. His mother had insisted he wear the crown of his father, so there would be no mistaking it was now his, in spite of his unheeded arguments that he should have his own. Many lords had brought their unmarried daughters to court, and these ladies, fair and fowl, all kept watch on the young king with hopeful eyes. When he should catch one appraising him, the common thing was to coyly avert her eyes from him, but he knew without mistake that he was the center of interest, and hoped he measured to expectation.

Mortimer was in the company of his own wife, Joan of Geneville, a decidedly plain woman with uneven features, though richly dressed. He introduced her to Isabella, who had her three other children with her, John, the king's brother of eleven, eight-year-old Eleanor and her own Joan, just seven.

"May I present my lady wife, Joan." It was the first time Isabella had faced her since her alliance with Mortimer.

"Oh, the same name as my youngest," Isabella pushed her young daughter forward, perhaps as a barrier between them. Little Joan curtsied politely, but even at her age understood as well as any at court the chasm between them. It was even clear upon this occasion Isabella's relation to Mortimer was no secret to his wife, and even more that he benefitted from it.

"Mortimer speaks well of your management of his lands while he is at court. Your father was the Lord of Trim and Ludlow?" Isabella asked in conversation of feigned interest.

"Yes. He died without sons and his lands fell to me." It was unspoken that Mortimer had gained much of his position by his marriage to the wealthy dower. His wife had lingered as prisoner in her family's Welsh castle at Skipton while he was imprisoned in the tower, but sent home to the Eire counties of Meath upon the coronation.

"I do not envy your crossing. The sea to Ireland I hear is chill to the bone." The pleasantries between them were as icy as the Irish sea. Mortimer had not called for his wife to be reunited, but to make supplication to the new king.

"I must offer my gratitude to your Highness for the generosity you have shown my husband and our family."

Isabella smiled at her, little betraying her true satisfaction. "It pleases me then, that you find our friendship beneficial."

Joan tried her best to smile in return, but found it tightening into something else. Mortimer nodded for his wife to depart. She curtsied in duty and whisked away to join her children.

Mortimer's mind was occupied with the other purpose for which he had brought his wife and family to the occasion. He stood with Isabella, watching her son dance with the girls presented by their fathers.

"The boy should take a wife," he said casually. "It would keep him occupied with home matters."

"It would seem my handsome son has no end of suitors. Who would make a good match is the question."

"Any one of my own unwed daughters would make an excellent spouse, and would keep our alliance close."

His wife had joined a group of four aging young women who seemed to have received all the worst physical traits of their family line. Isabella was diplomatically silent. And she perhaps had her own alliances in mind.

As Edward danced with one ardent young maiden, she whispered in his ear, making a very unladylike suggestion. His eyes grew wide and his face flushed.

He excused himself, but as he made his bow, his eyes fell upon a girl he had not noticed before, standing near the fire. He was transfixed. The flame light danced on the delicate skin of the girl's cheek and her tawny golden hair almost seemed to glow like the sun. And this girl did not look away in false modesty like the others. She met his gaze with cool curiosity until he was the one forced to look away.

A lord stepped near with his daughter, but Edward passed him without notice, walking across the hall to the beautiful girl with the unflinching eyes.

"Maiden, would you dance with a king?" he asked with the swagger of confidence gained from his certainty as the center of all attention.

The girl curtsied politely.

"No, my lord, I would not." Her speech had the clipped accent of Flanders, one of the visiting foreigners of the low lands.

"And why not?" he asked, with some puzzlement. He had never been refused before. "Is my dancing not to your liking?"

"Your capers are fair passing." She offered with faint praise.

Edward was confounded, "Are my features displeasing, then?"

"No, my lord, your face is not objectionable. Except for the pimples, perhaps."

Edward quickly touched his face to find the blemishes, but there were none and the girl broke into a soft laugh.

"You mock me!"

"Forgive me," she apologized. "It is only Your Grace's vanity I mock. You wear a crown so unfitting you must hold it with your hand, yet, you would still be King if you set it aside."

Edward considered the crown gripped awkwardly in his hand, that he had never really wanted to wear but for his mother's insistence.

"Then, if I took off my crown, would you dance with me?"

The girl made a gasp, but only in jesting mockery, "Oh no, I could not dance with such a meek king who so easily forfeits his crown!"

Edward stood taller as if he might overcome her objection with his station, "Then, would you dance with a king who tomorrow risks his life to lead fifty thousand men to battle for the honor of his country?"

"Oh, no," she replied, "I could not dance with so boastful a king! How brave is it to take such a huge army with wagons and tents against a small band of Scotsmen who carry only oatmeal and tin plates?"

"Oh, you—' He was at last without riposte in their duel. "You vex me!"

"Then, Your Majestic Grace should excuse me, for I cannot wish to cause you discomfort." And so she curtsied and made to turn away. "My lord."

He could not let her escape and pulled the full force of his rank.

"Stop! You must dance with me! I command it as your king!"

She did stop and turned back to him, fixing him with pleased amusement, then curtsied again in all due deference.

"But you are not my king. I am from Hainaut. My liege is the French king. I am surprised my lord, that you do not recognize me."

Edward paused in frustrated uncertainty. She did seem familiar to him and it was only now that who she was came to him. He had played with her on a brief visit to the court of her father in Valenciennes when his mother had gone to beg her cousin's support against her husband. Her name was Philippa, he remembered well now, but she had been such an ungainly girl then, now nearly four eventful years ago. She was much changed.

"Pardon," she said, taking her leave and stepping away from him again.

Edward was now completely at a loss to action. He should have recognized her, and now he had insulted her forever. And she had insulted him, not in manners or action, but well, in besting him in the duel between men and women. The company around all watched the odd behavior of the young monarch as he stomped and paced.

"Bury!" Edward called out loudly.

Richard Bury appeared at Edward's side, pushing through the crowd. He was now much more man than the fellow boy Edward had decked in the White Tower courtyard. He had been made the royal prince's tutor, transported to the court in France with his mother's retinue at Edward's request to give him familiar company in foreign lands and had become the young king's closest friend. He somewhat amused himself at his younger master's plight.

"Richard, she will not dance with me. What should I do?"

Richard shrugged, amused at his youthful plight. "You are King. Cut off her head."

Edward pondered a moment, still pacing, wondering if he might. Though, such a remedy would take a trial and full proclamation of the cause and charge, and so be as embarrassing as the eyes now all trained upon him. He noticed something on the floor and picked it up. It was a stocking tie. A thin-edged silk with Dutch embroidered lace.

"The lady has lost a garter," Richard noted.

Edward quickly thrust his crown into Richard's hands.

"Hold the thing!" he commanded, in that sudden decision of emotion the tutor had come to see familiar in him, a fiery intent that would lead to impetuous action which could not be deterred.

Edward strode to one of the royal guards standing watch in the hall and drew the sword from the soldier's scabbard, hefting it in his hands. Then, as all the host observed, he walked across the hall with the sword blade, until he came to Philippa, talking with some ladies, her back turned.

They all stared uneasily as the fiery young king marched up with the naked sword. Philippa noticed their shock and turned to face him. Edward immediately turned the sword point to the stone floor, standing it in front of himself as he bent to one knee. He draped the garter around the pommel.

"Lady, you have lost a garter. You have angered me enough, I should keep it and use it as a saddle tie for my horse. But as I am a knight and hope to be gallant, I here return it to you."

The gathered ladies and squires near looked askance, and all the company had heard.

"And shame on any who think ill of it," he added.

Philippa discreetly checked under her surgown and indeed one of her woolens drooped on her ankle. It was her turn to be embarrassed as the ladies around her giggled.

"And if you but dance one measure with me in return, I will decree an order of knighthood to rival that of Arthur's round table, to be formed in your honor. I shall call it the Order of the Garter. What do you say?"

"Order of the Garter?" Philippa giggled as she looked into his intense blue Plantagenet eyes, the drama and his tendency to grand ideas she had come to know in their childish play familiar to her, and welcome.

She made a grand curtsy. "For all this, my lord, I shall say you are a silly king." Then she offered a sweet smile. "Yet, I will dance a measure with you, if only to get you off your knobby knee. And you may keep the silk as my token, if it pleases you."

The young Edward glowed. And they did dance a measure, and more.

It would be many years before Edward would fulfill his pledge of a grand order of chivalry and many repetitions of this event would be told and embellished by friends and enemies. The king would have many enemies in the fullness of time, some of his own making, and some who would soon to intend to bring him down, but for this night the gesture would belong to them alone.

Edward remained in Philippa's company, not leaving her side for much of the rest of the celebration, with all other hopeful fathers forlorn for their daughters, lost in dashed hope. Mortimer was among them as he observed the king and the flaxen-haired girl from across the channel sea while they listened to a balladeer sing of St George's conquest of the dragon while a fool acted the story in comical mime. Philippa laughed at the fool's antics and grasped Edward's arm with delight.

With Mortimer were his two squire sons, both soon to reach their majority, William and Henry. They, too, took notice of the boy with the crown too big for his head and the winsome youthful lady upon his arm.

Mortimer pushed his way across the hall to interrupt Edward, offering a deference he rarely would, unless it served his intent. "Your Grace."

"Lord Mortimer, isn't this celebration magnificent?" Edward was full in joy.

Mortimer smiled at the boy's innocence, and cautioned, "Celebration may be premature. We have not yet won the campaign."

"But it cannot last long, with God, and fearsome warriors like you on our side."

Mortimer made a small bow. "My lord turns my head. Won't you introduce me to the lady who keeps you company?"

"Lord Roger Mortimer of Wigmore, the Maid Philippa of Hainaut."

Mortimer needed no introduction, knowing too well who she was.

"Sweet pleasure." Mortimer bowed and Philippa curtsied to him, but he quickly ignored her and pulled Edward aside with a familiar arm about his shoulder.

"I would ask a boon, Edward. My squire sons, Henry and William, stand ready for knighthood. It would honor me greatly if you would lay the sword upon them with your own hand."

Philippa felt abandoned as Mortimer steered Edward away from her. She allowed herself to be pulled to dance by an eager squire, but peered past him to watch as Edward was introduced to Mortimer's sons by their father.

Edward's attention was only half upon the Mortimer brothers, the other half seeking out Philippa and spotted her dancing with another. When she noticed him looking, she turned away with theatrical disinterest. Disappointed, but too proud to show it, Edward also turned from her. If she could so easily choose another, he was king, and there were many more who would gladly dance with him.

And Mortimer was satisfied.

5

The clatter of horse hooves and boots echoed off the cobblestones through the narrow streets of York. A stream of the army's vanguard stretched in rows behind the portcullis of Monk Gate. The main body of the army, the foot soldiers, archers and wagons waited outside the wall for the order to march.

Isabella was worried for her son's first test in battle, but Mortimer had assured her he would be kept away from the most dangerous action. The boy's command would be purely ceremonial, and the first ceremony was to bestow Mortimer's two eldest sons with knighthood. Edward touched his sword to the shoulders of kneeling Thomas and William before the host of the king's knights in glinting armor and flags below the high spires of the Minster. After they kissed the sword, he mounted his horse, with sunlight flaring on his regal boy-sized armor, taking his place just ahead of his uncles, Edmund and Lancaster. Mortimer mounted his black steed just behind them, with his new anointed sons beside him.

The column of brightly surcoated knights were followed by the lancers and pikemen, and painted wagons with the coat-of-arms of their owners emblazoned on the cloth covers. Only a portion of the army could be glimpsed at once. Ladies gathered on the great wall battlements of York and other high places to watch them depart for glory, waving their kerchiefs. Among them, Isabella had climbed the levels of the Monk Gate to the lookout wall to view down to her son. Edward searched the battlement for Philippa, but could not find her.

Mortimer urged his horse from his place to the side of the king, forcing Edmund to a position just behind him.

"Do you look for someone? Your mother? She is there." Mortimer pointed to where Isabella stood proudly, but it was not for his mother he was searching. Edward slumped in his saddle and angrily ripped the silk garter from the hilt of his sword, ready to throw it to the ground. Yet, he looked up one last time before he would dash the symbol, and now could see Philippa on the wall, pressing through a crowd of other ladies. She smiled and waved a kerchief. Edward's spirit soared and he rose in his saddle, holding the garter in his hand to signal the column to march.

"Mighty God, bless us this day and grant our triumph be swift!" he shouted. And so, with his agile mind filled with visions of glory, and heart filled with the thrilling new discovery of love, the boy king led his army to battle.

The army started forward, clattering on the stones as flags waved in the breeze of drifting clouds. As Edward looked again to Philippa, he was filled with warmth for the adventure ahead and broke his horse into a canter and then a gallop. The rest of the knights were taken by surprise, riding out after him in his enthusiasm, with the foot soldiers hurrying to keep up.

Yet, the gloried expectations of battle triumphs too soon turned to the mire of war's reality.

6

The burned pastures of Northumberland were muddy with rains. Archers tugged at the heavy wagons which had become bogged. The once brightly colored coats of the knights were stained with muck. After three months campaign Edward's great army had come to a standstill.

Edward gathered his commanders in his tent for council, Lancaster, Edmund, and Mortimer were his chief advisors with the largest of the forces.

The tent flap opened and Montagu ducked in from the drizzling gloom.

"Your Grace, there be sixteen wagons with broken axles, and fighting has started again between our bowmen and the Zeeland speakers. They can't even understand each other's insults."

Edward banged his small fist on the table. "And where are the Scots?! We move at snail's pace while they strike where they please."

"We are fifty-thousand strong," Mortimer tried to calm him. "They cannot escape us long."

Edward was not calmed. He had led his great army with Mortimer's experienced guidance only to arrive time after time at one sacked village after the next. "They have done so for more than three months! They laugh at me from the mists." He turned away from the table, stepping to a corner of the tent, hiding his face so that his elders might not see the mist in his own eyes.

Mortimer made show to Lancaster, "I hold myself at fault. The boy is beyond his years. I should not have allowed him generalship."

Lancaster begrudgingly nodded agreement, though he knew it was not the young king who had chosen their course.

Edmund joined Edward, who silently stared with wet eyes at his crown helm and resting armor set aside, putting a consoling hand on his shoulder.

"Be less hard on yourself. This is the baptism of your first campaign and you have only followed your elder advisors."

"We have a mighty force, but our size has not served us!" Edward allowed his mind to search the thoughts which had pulled at him as they had marched from village to village where the raiding Scots had struck, only to find burned barns and fields. They had only met skirmishes with a few scouts and had seen almost no battle at all.

"Perhaps we are too strong?" he said to his uncle, but speaking so his other advisors might hear.

"Too strong?" Edmund wondered what he meant.

Edward was filled with a sudden new energy. He could see clearly, as if the fog had lifted from his own mind. He returned to the planning table and his gathered elders.

"If the Scots can move on only oatmeal and grazing cattle, then why not we?!" He looked to the map of the land spread before them, with the many pieces representing the positions of his great army and the small markers of the enemy. "I say we take a small force of knights on swift horse and leave the fat behind."

Mortimer was taken at his surprise, "But Edward, this is a boy's whimsy!" he cautioned. "Would you waste such a great army?"

"You would be without tent and cook," Lancaster warned.

Edward saw it clearly and was not dissuaded. "What can I care for my own comfort when my soldiers' toes rot in their boots!"

Mortimer tried to assert his will. "This cannot be allowed, Edward! Patience is the wiser course."

Edward faced Mortimer. Would he do as he was bid as in the years past when he was a boy and ruled by others, or would he take his place among men? He stepped to the map on the table, spying it over to find the focus of his thought.

"No, it is time to act. By my command, tomorrow we cross the River Tyne." He pointed to a squiggling line on the map. "Here at Hawick. The remainder of our army will march to Carlisle to draw them from our scent."

Mortimer held his anger at being defied. He looked to the others for their support, but they seemed taken with the boldness of the idea.

"Sire. As you wish." Mortimer bowed in duty and strode from the tent.

Mortimer stood on a bulwark of the English camp, watching the fading of the day, as if the fading of his own ambition. He was joined by his sons, who had heard the order.

"He defies you, father?" Henry, the eldest, asked of him.

"He is king, he may have his way." Mortimer said with proper politic, but did not reveal his true feelings.

A messenger hurriedly climbed to find him, summoned.

"You sent for me, Lord Mortimer?" he said as he stood waiting for direction. Mortimer handed him a folded paper sealed by unmarked wax.

"Ride out and find the Douglas. My name will give you safety."

The messenger nodded and slipped off into the dark.

Waiting until he had disappeared once again into the night shadows, Mortimer confided his feeling to his newly knighted son. "If our young general seeks a true taste of war, perhaps he should have it."

Edward set out with twenty of his best knights and their squires, along the south of the River Tyne to find ford while his main force moved west toward the border city of Carlisle. His fast cadre found a broken stream in a rocky glen they made to cross, but as Edward and his full armored knights forged through the rushing waters of the rain-swollen river, suddenly quarrel arrows from crossbows flew upon them from the rocks on the hills above. Horses cried as their riders fell into the rushing water and sank in their heavy armor, tumbling down the rocky stream.

Montagu, Edmund, and several other knights reaching the opposite bank charged up into the rocks, but the Scotsmen had already gone into the mists, and would not stand for a battle. Edward crossed and met them.

"They vanish like the wind," Edmund said in heavy breath.

"We haven't seen them for weeks, yet they lie in wait when we cross!" Edward spun his horse and looked upon the landscape. He wondered if he had made a mistake.

"I smell some mischief, Nephew." Edward turned his horse to his uncle. Could someone have revealed their plan? He turned his horse again to watch as squires dragged a drowned knight from the river stream.

"In any case, we have lost any advantage of surprise," said Edward, thinking to adjust his intent. "We have crossed. We will gain as much ground as we can before nightfall. Our suppliers must catch us."

"Surely, you would wait for your tent, Edward." Mortimer advised.

Edward thought of it. For three years past in halls of palaces and surrounded by the protection of saluting swords he would have listened to Mortimer's counsel and obeyed, but he was now in an open field with men he had asked to follow him.

"No. If we wait for our wagons, the raiders will pick at us." he reasoned. "We must move on. I'll sleep in my spurs as those I command."

He turned on his horse to shout to all the company who could hear him, to the squires and cartage bearers, "I'll make a knight with a hundred acres of land any squire that brings me news of the Scots hiding place!"

"Hya!" He spurred his horse, spinning the steed and charging up the river slope at the gallop.

The king's small force rode until the set of the sun without again setting eyes on a Scotsman in arms. The weary knights pulled up their horses on a grassy hillside as the orange sun set in the Scottish mist.

Edward would have gone on to midnight, but Edmund counseled his nephew to stop, "This ground looks pillowy enough. Perhaps by morning, we'll have word of the kilts."

The knights dismounted and searched for the most comfortable spots before laying out on the grassy slope in their armor, holding their horses' reins in gauntleted fists.

Edward found a spot under a spreading oak and tried to find a comfortable position on the bumpy ground in his rattling armor, perhaps wishing he'd not been so gallant.

Mortimer, lying nearby, could hear the discomforted sound of the young king's armor. He took some satisfaction that the boy may be learning a hard lesson and closed his eyes.

Finally, Edward gave up hope of a soft rest and lay as still as he could, listening to the chirping of crickets and night sounds. Even they faded into the silence of the drifting fog.

Edward still laid, shivering with the cold to his bones in the damp, unable to sleep, when he noticed the cracking of twigs. Two figures came from the fog, picking their way among the sleeping knights.

Edward was startled by a hand shaking him. He struggled in his armor, unable to sit up, surprised to find Richard Bury with another boy.

"Edward, are you asleep?" Richard asked.

Edward looked at him as if he might be joking.

"We've found the Scots!" Richard said excitedly. "This squire Rokeby did, but was too shy to tell you."

Edward struggled to sit up, but could not rise with them. The two squires hid their amusement. Edward held out his arms.

"Don't just stand there. Get me up!"

Richard and the squire, Thomas of Rokeby, aided the young king to rise to his feet.

"As your sovereign king, I make you both knights this day!"

With fresh news of an encampment of Scottish raiders, the king's force mounted at the dawn and made for an early attack. Skirmishes with small bands of Scotsmen lasted through the day, with conflict and retreat and conflict again. By near nightfall, Edward's cadre found the main body of the Scots at the side of a riverlet.

Edward's knights clashed with Scots knights with their clan kilts. A Scots knight maneuvered near to Edward and engaged him with his heavy Claymore sword. Edward defended as best he could with his own boy-sized weapon. Edmund saw his nephew engaged and charged his horse between the king and his attacker, hitting the Scottish knight with an arm blow that almost unseated him from his horse.

The Scot turned and rode to the river. The others also quickly retreated across the stream, fading into the woods and the short-lived battle was over.

"A captured kilter tells us they have run out of food and grow weary," Montagu reported with regained hope, "And our supplies have come. A good rest should make us fresh for the final assault."

Edward was exhilarated at his first real battle, tasting success. "Then we make after them in the morning." He met his uncle's hopeful mood. "I can smell a victory! Can't you?"

Edmund felt his nephew's enthusiasm. "Fortune does seem to smile, at last."

At Weardale, near the village of Stanhope, Edward's expeditionary army made camp. The supply wagons had joined them with two hundred men-at-arms sent from the main western force at Durham.

Edward's armor was laid aside as he knelt in front of a Father Chaplain, saying prayers. The chaplain blessed him and he stretched out on his cot, exhausted.

"I shall be nearby if you need me in the night, Sire," the father offered and bent from the tent.

The camp was dark and peaceful. The newly arrived forces were as tired from fast march as Edward's knights from their skirmishes. An owl hoot punctuated the night. From the woods across a small stream of the River Wear, a sentry heard hushed voices.

"Ho, the watchword?!" the sentry shouted.

A voice echoed back from the woods, "St. George!"

The sentry relaxed his guard, sitting back down to eagerly finish his salted beef.

Suddenly, the stillness was shattered when horsed Scotsmen leaped from the woods and splashed across the river. They shouted like banshees. The knight in the lead wore the black armor and colors of the Douglas clan.

The Scotsmen shouted as they rode into the heart of the camp, "St. George! St. George!" But the cry was as much mockery as it was a feigned password.

Edmund threw back his tent flap with his sword in hand. The Scottish knight from the day's earlier clash rode at him, but he dodged the charge and deftly cut the knight from his horse. The dead Scot tumbled from his saddle onto a tent.

The Black Douglas rode through the tents with one target in his mind. He found the king's banner and jumped from his horse.

Edward was asleep when Douglas burst in. The mighty lord, enemy of his father and his father before him, raised his sword to strike down on the third of his name, but Edward, awakened by the rattle of Douglas' scabbard, rolled off the cot as the blade came down, chopping the bed in two.

Near to naked, Edward scrambled to his armor, drawing his sword and just managed to block a blow by Douglas. Douglas swung again and knocked the shakily held sword from his hands. Douglas raised his sword over the now defenseless boy.

"Have your lesson, young master English," he growled. But as the blade came down, the chaplain rushed in.

"God's Mercy!" he cried as he threw himself on top of Edward. The sword killed the priest, while Edward laid helpless underneath.

"The king is attacked!" voices shouted outside.

While Douglas was distracted by the shouting of the English, Edward crawled from under the priest and rolled underneath the edge of the tent, before the fearsome Scots lord could strike again.

The Black Douglas swept from the inside the king's tent and leaped onto his horse while all around his fellow Scotsmen fought with the awakened knights.

Mortimer emerged from his own tent, already dressed in full armor with his sons, as if bravely prepared for battle, yet, too late for an attack so swiftly concluded, as was its object. Douglas met Mortimer's dark-eyed gaze from the back of his horse and gave a soldier's bow of common recognition, before turning the animal to ride back toward the river, shouting as he rode.

"O'Douglas! O'Douglas!"

The rest of the Scots followed him into the night, leaving the English knights confused and bewildered. Edward sunk down next to the body of his dead chaplain. He looked to God above and cried in a boy's abject frustration. Mortimer could scarce hide his satisfaction at Edward's humiliation. A lesson taught and well learned, he thought.

The settlement of the war would take nearly a year to negotiate, during which time the boy would grow. The Scots were to pay thirty-thousand marks for invading the border and England's kings would relinquish their last sovereign claim on the highland land. Edward's youngest sister, Joan, only seven, would marry the new Scottish king, David, but five years old, and the two thrones would be joined in future heirs. The great Robert de Brus, called the Bruce, had died while his probing warriors had harried the English king. William Douglas would carry the heart of the dead king in a box on Crusade, but would die himself in a battle against the Moors in Spain before he could reach Jerusalem.

A royal wedding was held in the dank ancient abbey of Scone with heavy Roman arches, where the child bride and child husband held hands, kneeling before the altar of Scone. The boy, David, the fresh king of the Scots, in bright burnished child's crowned armor, cried through the whole ceremony. The only ones who smiled were Mortimer and Isabella, who had gained from the payments.

Edward's younger brother, John, born at Eltham, seeing his brother crowned king, and his younger sister now made Queen of Scotland, was petulant at his lowly place, so at the age of twelve, was granted the new-created title, Duke of Cornwall, though he had never set foot upon that shire. Edward liked his little brother, of energetic character despite an ague of the lungs which caused him a wheezing breath whenever he exerted himself. Though regularly besting him at near all the games they played, Edward had resolved to let him win at every third try, to avoid filial acrimony. His wise-for-her-years sister, Eleanor, born at Woodstock, now reaching young womanhood, was sent to live in care of the widow of the Earl of Gloucester. Her charge by her mother was to learn the graces of her station 'til she might be wed to good advantage, and as well, to provide her mother with secret reports of the comings and goings of the household, as Isabel of Hastings was a Despenser daughter and in regular contact with the dissolute family who might be a danger.

And Edward, having little power under the Council of Regency, occupied himself with what matters he was allowed.

~~~

CHAPTER FIVE

1

16th Day of October, 1327

At Windsor, a band of young knights and squires in training in the bailey courtyard below the great Round Tower, some stripped to the waist, tilted at the jousting dummy, tossed the heavy stone to each other, or crossed dulled broad swords. Among them, a young man with a strong bare back sparred with an older Richard Bury at the quarterstaff. Edward was now sixteen years and much grown in stature and strength. He had sprouted a sparse beard of near blond color. His education in arts and Latin, law and the history of great houses from ancient times to his own had been full, though his lessons in politics and maneuver would take some time more to complete. Richard had been his teacher in many of these and his good friend, and though an anointed knight, slight of build and not a warrior. Edward delivered Richard a swift flurry of thwacks with the staff and knocked him into the trout pond. Richard bobbed for air.

"I yield to Your Majestic Grace. God speaks thunder in your mighty staff." Richard bowed with a wet show in the water. He was also the young king's counselor in humility.

"Flatterer." Edward laughed as he pulled his wet friend from the pond.

A loud clapping echoed from the bailey walk above the courtyard. Mortimer peered down on them. He had been watching.

"His Majestic Grace is much improved," he said from high above.

Edward whispered to Richard, "It seems everyone is full of flattery today."

"But I see the boy still plays with wooden sticks."

"Would you cross steel with me, then, Lord Mortimer?" Edward offered with a slight bow.

Mortimer smiled. "By your command," and made his way to the bailey stairs.

"My lord's victory has gone to his head,' Richard joked, knowing Mortimer's prowess.

"You think I cannot make a good showing?" Edward asked.

Richard smiled. "The king is dead, long live the king." He softly hummed a funeral dirge as Mortimer joined Edward in the swords list boundary box.

Edward selected a sword from the practice box and his shield with the Plantagenet three lions embossed on the hardened leather. Mortimer selected a long, two-handed sword but ignored the shields.

Edward observed him. "Do you think so little of my skill, Lord Mortimer, you take no shield?"

"You've grown since your last birthday. But I have several stone and many years on you. I wish you an even chance."

"Then, have on and let's see if your years serve you well."

Edward saluted and took his stance. Without salutation, Mortimer swung his sword. Edward barely blocked the blow, and the swords rang across the courtyard. The fight was on as swords clanged and clashed in a swift flurry. They broke apart, moving around the box, sizing for an opening.

"Your skill with sword has also improved," Mortimer offered.

Edward nodded thanks at the compliment. There was another flurry of blows until they separated again. Edward took the moment of close intimacy to question the lord who ruled him.

"Mortimer, you have influence with my mother and the Council. What parlay has passed of when I may assume the full rights of my reign?"

Mortimer laughed, "Patience. You are but sixteen! You have shown a good account at politic, I'll admit. Creating the office of Justice-Of-The-Peace for petty squabbles was fair kingship. Let your mind be occupied with like ideas, but leave matters of statecraft for the more experienced."

Edward had indeed in his forming years since his coronation spent his thoughts on justice as he had learned his Latin and of the formation and fall of great Rome and Greece before, and the justice courts of the great Charles. He had convinced the Parliament and Royal Council to form a system of small courts where an appointed magistrate might sit in the king's stead to hear grievances of the people which might be settled with an even judgment. Mortimer had little care for these matters and had paid his attention more on what lord might be granted more land, or less. The common people were of small concern to his plans.

"If the settlement with the Scots is the example of experience, perhaps were better to give inexperience its chance," Edward joked.

Mortimer flushed with sudden anger and swung a furious cut which bashed against Edward's shield, making him step back.

Edward was surprised by the fury behind the strike. "I did not intend to criticize, or offend, my lord. I only question the value gained."

"Then, I take no offense. A boy's place is to question." Mortimer calmed his outward manner, for he had an object in his mind to discuss, yet, still exalted in his pride. "How else may youth learn?"

Mortimer made a thrust that caught Edward slightly on the hip. Edward made a quick feint to draw Mortimer to parry, then quickly countered and caught

Mortimer on the leg with a touch. Mortimer, surprised, nodded acknowledgement of the coup.

"Have you given thought to taking a wife, Edward?" he asked. "Now you begin to thrive in battle arts it, would serve to have a male heir should some misfortune befall."

Edward looked to his wrist where Philippa's garter was still tied, now worn with time and sweat. "Yes. I have been thinking of it."

"Your Mother and I have gone to some pains in making an appropriate choice." Mortimer offered, easing to his point. "It's hard for a father to choose between his daughters which is the most suitable, but we have come to a determination."

Edward winced at the thought, for he had seen the Mortimer daughters.

"I appreciate your pains, Sir, but you should know, I have in mind another."

Mortimer's anger returned and he flew back with a flurry, battering against Edward's sword and shield, until a final two-handed stroke knocked him out of the training box into the dirt. Mortimer bashed the shield out of his grip and stood over him, pressing his sword point to Edward's chin.

"I yield to your age and skill, my lord," Edward fixed him with a challenging eye, "but I do intend to have some say at least in my choice of queen."

Mortimer tossed his dull-bladed sword aside and made a small courtesy before striding away. Richard helped Edward up, and they watched Mortimer curiously.

"He seems to feel some heat in the matter," observed Richard.

"Yes. But would you marry one of his homely brood?"

"Not for all his growing lands and titles." They laughed, but Richard turned serious. Mortimer, with Isabella's agreement, had placed before the council and Edward for his signing, a distribution of lands to strengthen the Welsh Marcher lords and his allies, taking for himself Wallingford Castle and proposing that he be granted the title Earl of the March.

"The Regency Council denies him nothing. Even the money from the Scots found its way to Mortimer's pockets."

Edward was worried about it, but he still held Mortimer as an advisor and mentor. "Whispers are not equal to proof. He has been a good friend."

Richard was curious at his forgiveness of Mortimer and watched Edward playing with the garter on his wrist. He knew his mind. "Have you approached your mother about marrying Philippa?"

Edward shook his head, uneasy at the thought. Convincing his mother to turn away from Mortimer's desire would require a good argument, but he knew an avenue which held a stronger pull on her than her paramour.

"Well, you'd better make haste, or you'll find yourself calling Mortimer, 'Papa'!"

In the Queen Mother's chambers at Windsor, a room full of lady's maids flitted about Isabella, for she needed more and more to tend her needs now that her war had been won and the battle had turned to that which comes to all in time's march. While they carefully wrapped her hair in a silk net, she checked her skin in a hand mirror. She noticed a new wrinkle at the edge of her eye and scolded a maid in French, making her hurry to get the seal oil to repair the damage.

Edward tapped on the door and walked in without waiting for a response. He had thrown a loose chemise over his sweaty shoulders and the maids could not help a blushing giggle.

"Maman, je voidrais un petit privee." He spoke in French, as he always did when he wanted something intimate from her favor.

"If you speak in your English, my ladies will not understand and I may continue dressing." She had drawn all her hand maids from across the channel sea, the better to keep rumors from passing to the English masters who might want to know her secrets.

He kissed her cheek and she kissed the palm of his hand, then frowned as she found blisters there. Edward pulled his hand away.

"I think it's time I married."

"And what fine lady will have you with rough callused hands?"

He looked curiously through the box of beauty oils and powders the maids worked from.

"I'm not sure I want so fine a lady she must spend all her days tending her appearance."

Isabella was cool. "In the life we live, a woman's appearance is her currency. If she spends it unwisely, she is doomed to end her days in poverty." She shooed him away from her essentials and he hoisted himself onto the window ledge, dangling his feet.

"Then, perhaps it's best to think of a purely political match. What do you think of an alliance with the house of Hainaut?"

They had discussed it before, but she had been pressed by other counsel. "But a selection has been already made for you. Mortimer's eldest."

"I forget, is she the one with the crossed eyes and crooked nose, or the one with the shape of the ball in the Italian bowling game?"

"Shush!" she scolded, hiding her own amusement. She was not unfamiliar with the issue. "Fairness of the face and figure is not all in these matters." She made a closer examination of the now oiled wrinkle in her mirror.

"But would you force on me so 'impoverished' a bride? Your cousin has served well in war. A marriage would be just reward. And ships would be needed should we turn toward France."

Isabella thought about it, but tried to hold her ground, "I have made the promise."

"But the lands of Hainaut would add to our holdings on the French continent. It would be helpful if we press our claim on your father's throne. The Flemish ports and flat plains would make for a swift approach to Paris if arms were called."

Isabella, the warrior queen, liked this argument but shook it off. She had by now, had enough of swords, but her cousin, wed to the Lord of Hainaut was her closest ally among the Valois. Edward hopped from the window ledge to sit close at his mother's feet. He would press the advantage.

Isabella waved her maids away and they scurried from the chamber. She played with her son's sweat-tangled hair.

"Vous etes tres humide." It was rare now that they were only mother and son, and not rulers in court maneuver. She noticed the garter tied around his wrist.

"My Hainaut cousin has three daughters. Is there one who habits your mind?"

Edward tried to be casual. "No. But now that you ask me to think of it, Philippa does have a delicate eye. If I remember."

His interest in favoring her was no secret to his mother. "Philippa? She is the youngest of bearing age. No, it cannot be the youngest. This would give insult to the father. A delegation must be sent to make the choice, if this alliance is to be pressed."

"A delegation!?"

"Oui. The Bishop of Northborough, I think, will be good to send."

"A delegation." Edward tried to resign himself to more maneuver, but at least he had turned her from Mortimer's plan.

"But can I choose my own proxy for the solemnizing?" he asked.

She silently nodded her ascent, looking again to her mirror.

Edward rose from the floor, privately rejoicing at half the battle won. "What of Lord Mortimer?"

Isabella allowed herself an impish smirk. She had not forgotten the girl who had won the favor of all the court in times past. "I will find means to console him." She checked the bones of her corset and placed the collar of her bodice just so.

Edward was made uncomfortable when his mother took this tone. He didn't like to think of his mother with Mortimer in private. "And what consoling has my father in his tower keep?"

"Non!" was her sharp and instant reply. Another familiar argument.

"I have not seen him in nearly two years!" Edward pleaded. His father had been held in an apartment at Kenilworth under Lancaster's care since he signed away his crown, but his children had all been kept from him. When Edward's case to visit his father had been pressed, he was removed from Lancaster's supervision and moved to the castle of the Berkeleys, Mortimer's ally in Gloucester. "I am old enough he cannot affect me in some evil way."

"He abandoned his wife and his children for unnatural pleasure. Let him eat the fruit of his desire. He stays at Berkeley and there he will remain. My son also may choose. If he returns to his father, he loves not his mother."

Edward returned to the bailey yard where Richard waited to hear the outcome of his mission.

"How went your pleadings?" he asked.

"Half the campaign." Edward said, still thinking of the next step. "My mother sends a delegation to Hainaut. It seems, if I am to ever have my own will, I must work in secret. And you must be my agent."

"Do you have a plan?"

With a mischievous smile, Edward threw his arm around his friend's shoulder to lead him further from hearing ears and confided, "I do know the tastes of the old Bishop who will lead the choosing."

2

The Count of Hainaut held title to lands which spread from the river Hain to Charleroi as well as the lowlands of Holland to the North Sea at Amsterdam. His wife, Joan of Valois, was the sister of King Phillip, now on the throne of France, and cousin to Isabella. Marrying her son to a daughter of the Valois would only strengthen the ties between the royal lineages of the Fleur-de-Lis of France to the Lion of England, should Isabella press her claim on the throne of her father, to pass through her to the direct male of the line, her son Edward.

A marriage proxy party arrived at the castle of Valenciennes, charged to solemnize a marriage, but with no instruction as to which maiden of the house to be selected as a bride. The choice was to be left to the discretion of a delegation of prelates sent for the purpose.

Three English bishops were led by the muffin-faced, aged Bishop of Northborough. They had been sent to make the choice upon examination of the girls, all well known to the Queen Mother, their aunt, but upon whom no-one of the English court had laid eyes in three years. To marry a cousin, a dispensation was needed from the Pope, and had been given at some cost to the treasury, and the daughters were assembled in the presence of their mother and Count William. Richard had been included in the party at Edward's urging, with no standing of office but charged by the king to act as his voice.

The three eligible daughters, Philippa, Johanna, and Isabel, were gathered in the hall with their attendants. The courtier nobles stood in attendance, the most aged and infirm of among them allowed to lean against the wall, where they might endure the ceremony, but away from the present sight of the principal lords. The family had already made one important alliance through the marriage of a child. The eldest daughter, Margaret, had already been wed to the German Holy Roman Emperor Ludwig of Bavaria. A second daughter wed to a king would cement the lowlands as a broker of power far larger than their holdings.

The girls were all attractive, but the last to enter the hall, Philippa, now fifteen years, outshone her siblings. And she was attended by only one serving maid, where her elder sisters each had at least five. Whether this was by her true nature or by her design for this occasion is a mystery. Perhaps she had been given some suggestion in advance of the thoughts in discussion among the delegation.

Count William formed his girls into a line before the committee. Much discussion and consideration had already been made, and a decision was near, but the prelates still had not come to a choice. Northborough was yet to settle himself. Richard, who as the king's ear had been present in all the deliberations, could see that the old man was endeavoring not to ogle the young tender girls, perhaps regretting his own vow of chastity made so many years ago, and never broken, unlike so many other priests of his class.

Richard sidled near to Philippa that he might pass a message from Edward. "My lord sends his regards," he whispered, "and bid me give you this." He subtly presented her with the garter Edward had kept.

She examined the dirty silk with cold eyes. "He returns my token in such a filthy state? Is this meant as a sign of his ill regard for me?"

Richard was surprised at her reaction. He had known her briefly at York in the company of his master when she was thirteen and had witnessed her ability to spar with a sharp wit.

"No, Lady. It is intended as a sign of his love. He sends it in the hope you will return it to him with your own sweet hand."

"If he professes to love me, why does he send these leering ogres to parade us like cattle at sale?!" she said with a fire in her eye, determined to stake her feelings, "If your fickle king prefers one of my sisters, then let him have any he choose. I care not for his shallow love."

Richard had been given charge to act in diplomacy on his master's behalf, yet without any formal authority. It was only his reason and guile that could serve this mission, and his greatest challenge now, at the moment of truth, was easing the object of it.

"I pray you, cool thy fire, mistress," he pleaded in a hushed whisper so that others might not hear. "This delegation is the requirement of my lord's mother. He has sent me as his voice. As proxy, I have no official vote, but it is my charge to turn the tide of opinion. If I fail and one of your sisters returns in your place, I am banished on forfeit of my head."

Philippa finally smiled, judging his loyalty and taking a liking to him. "Then proxy well, Sir Richard. I would not wish Edward to be so harsh upon a good friend."

Richard returned to the delegation, who yet had different opinions. He stood beside Northborough who was beset by the differing opinions of his two brother Bishops, each who had settled on different elder daughters, each with their own land dowers as enticements to fruitful wedding matches. Richard whispered into Northborough's ear.

"Pardon my interruption, but has Your Grace remarked upon the suppleness of complexion of Philippa, the next youngest child?"

The Bishop looked upon her and she smiled sweetly at him, as Richard continued his persuasion. "And indeed, do you not think the sweetness of her disposition outshines her sisters?"

The old bishop was impressed, but not yet convinced. "But she may not bring as big a dowry as her elders. See, she has only one attendant, and this shows her poverty in her father's eyes."

"Perhaps it is because of her more natural beauty she needs less attending, and thus shows more a frugal nature than poverty," Richard argued. "The lands which the others would bring to a husband would surely be an attraction for a lesser lord, but our alliance is with the father's house. A small province would add little to the holdings of the king of our great realm."

"Frugality is a much wonted quality in these tight times." Northborough pondered Richard's reasoning. Richard knew that the bishop was intent on his own opinion being superior to his companion delegates.

"And Your Grace cannot but have remarked that the maid Philippa is the best built about the hips and would expect to bring forth many and hopeful progeny."

The old prelate could not now help to ogle the girl with less than Holy eyes but made a flustering attempt to regain himself. Yet, he turned to the rest of the delegation, now decided.

"Freres, in truth, I cannot but insist on the child who appears to me the most fair and fertile. It shall be Philippa, who bears her grandmother's name."

The others were surprised at his sudden announcement, but offered little argument. They were agreed. Richard winked at Philippa, his entreaty a success.

Northborough whispered of the next step. "Convention holds that we examine the girl for proof of chastity. But I fear these foreigners' youth may not maintain the moral character of our own, and I would not want to embarrass an ally."

The others nodded ascent, and Northborough announced to the hall company present, "Lord William of Hainaut, it is decided the virgin Philippa of your issue shall be the King's choice. It is our consensus also that we will forgive the usual test of maidenhood."

William nodded agreement, but Philippa's cooler nature returned. She stood forward to speak for herself.

"My lords, if you do not think my virgin's virtue worthy of the test, then take one of my sisters. I would not have my honor, or that of a kingly husband be held in question."

"But, my lady—" Northborough stammered.

"Let the examination be done. I will spread for your curious eyes now, or else I will not spread for your king." She turned and marched to a nearby antechamber, pulling at her skirts. The prelates exchanged bewildered glances, then followed, filing into the room with her father and mother. Though Philippa hated, as anyone might, that she must offer herself for such a test, she would not have her honor slandered that she had refused it.

Richard waited with the rest of the company, shocked himself at the girl's will. After a few moments, Northborough emerged from the room with a flushed red face.

"The delegation is sat— satisfied," he stammered, shakily mopping his brow. "Let the solemnizing follow. Might someone bring me water to drink? I feel warmly."

Richard smiled as the old man fanned himself with a corner of his robe.

~~~

CHAPTER SIX

1

24th Day of January, 1328

The arrival of Philippa of Hainaut in London was greeted with great ceremony and cheer by the people, for there was great hope in this marriage. The people had heard of her beauty and pleasant nature. She did not bring a household of foreign attendants with her as the king's mother and other foreign brides had before her, but chose from English families for her retinue. The king had been invested in London, and so that the whole of the people might share in glory of their monarchs, the wedding of the king would be held at York. The procession through the country had been lined with flowers brought by ship from the fields of Holland to brighten the snowy lanes with color.

The wedding at York Minster was glorious with Edward and Philippa in wedding regalia, side by side in the glow of a thousand candles as the Canterbury Archbishop pronounced the sacrament. Isabella stood to the side of the dais with Mortimer among the lords behind her. The Queen Mother's mood was unrevealing as the Archbishop turned to her and held out his hands. She stepped forward and, with a moment's hesitancy, reached to remove the queen's crown from her own head.

The Archbishop held the crown of the Queen of England over Philippa's bowed head as he said the words of invocation, before lowering it onto her brow. Edward and Philippa arose, wedded, and Edward turned his radiant bride for all to see and there followed a hushed silence. He turned her to face him and kissed both of her hands, then pulled her close and gently touched his lips to hers. It was then, the bells of the twin towers began to ring and the choir sang out. A cheer rose from gathered witnesses filling the nave of the great church and spread among the throngs gathered outside along the processional route.

The great wedding feast and three days of celebration were over. In a chamber of the king's wardrobe of the York royal castle, Philippa was now alone with only the hand attendant who had been her intimate companion since her birth, Leanore of Mons, whom she called Lea. Philippa had been undressed and now stood in only a lace-lined, sheer silk and linen shift. Lea checked the tie to see that it did not fall open of its own accord. A wind blew at the windowpanes, and snow from the ledge drifted inside.

Philippa crossed her arms in front of the protruding points under her shift.

"A chill night for such warm doings. My nips perk."

Lea slapped her hands away. "Leave. Will pleasure your lord the better. He has not an easy task ahead and will need encouragement to spur his ardor."

Philippa giggled and Lea with her, for there was one last ceremony to perform. With the joining of two great houses, no doubt must be left to remain of legitimacy.

In another anteroom of the king's chamber, Richard sat cross-legged on a table, alone with Edward, naked underneath his ermine lined winter robe, as he performed push-ups on the stone floor.

"Edward, Your Grace, do you prepare to bed your bride or tilt with her?" he asked with a wry mirth.

Edward collapsed on the floor, breathless. He had counted to two-hundred. He joked away his own nerves. "If this is to be a joust, then my lance needs be strong to fulfill my vow. I will not show weakness before mine enemies."

The door was opened by the elderly John of Walsingham, granted the office of Chamberlain to the King in reward for his good service to Isabella in her tribulations.

"Your Grace, the nuptial bed is prepared and the witnesses await," he announced.

The king's bedchamber was filled with spectators, as if to a tournament, gathered to witness. Mortimer, Isabella, Lancaster, Edmund of Kent, Orleton and nine other members of the Ruling Council, bishops and lords, Philippa's mother and father, and even visiting foreign ambassadors from the courts of France, Holy Roman Imperial Bavaria, and a Papal Ligation, were all present to confirm the consummation of the marriage. In lesser houses, a report and soiled linen might suffice, but there were great forces of challenged crowns across Europe for whom no message or mere pronouncement of sacrament would satisfy.

Phillip VI, Edward's second uncle, had taken the throne of France, and there were yet two Popes in a divided Catholic Church. Nicholas V, called by his enemies "anti-pope", sat in Rome supported by the Holy Roman Emperor Ludwig, married to the Hainaut's daughter Margaret, while John XXII, successor to the scourge of the Templars, Clement X, of the line of French Popes, sat in Avignon. So it was that no less than war and peace were balanced on the certainty of this conjugal joining.

Trying to look in command, Edward strode to the large bed garlanded with flowers and herbs for luck and fertility. The other door opened and Philippa emerged in a robe, seeming small and shy in the crowded room. She stepped to the opposite side of the bed and met Edward's eyes with a warm smile. Lea slipped the robe from her shoulders and untied the silk thread holding her shift together. As it fell away, there was a gasp in the room, but Philippa quickly slipped into the bed. Richard removed Edward's robe like a squire at the lists and Edward slipped into the bed, flexing his shoulders.

Some time elapsed as the wedded couple seemed to move under the heavy fur cover, yet nothing apparently had developed of consequence. Edward lay face to face on top of his bride in the proper position proscribed for the task, and her parts were remarkable, but nothing stirred. Perhaps it was under the eyes of so many waiting for his regal performance that Edward struggled. He even thought for a moment, with a stab of worry, that perhaps he had inherited his father's affliction. Yet, Philippa waited patiently.

"You look troubled, my husband. Am I not to your liking?" Philippa asked as if she might be to blame, and perhaps wondering as well about the stories of the father and the great discord it had caused between his mother and kingdom. She had no practice at this either and had only been told in the most meager of description what was supposed to occur.

The audience standing about the chamber even began to grow bored in expectation, with some turning to private discussion of other political matters, or personal interests they might share with one another. There even began a whispered complaint that the dispensation granted for the wedding of cousins given by the anti-pope would not be accepted by the French court should an heir press a claim to the throne of Paris.

Lancaster, who was the council's senior advisor to the king, fearing a lack of action could turn to argument, stepped up to the bed and bent to whisper. Perhaps the boy needed some instruction for his first encounter of the sort.

"Is something amiss, Your Grace?" he asked kindly, "Can we be of any aid?"

"Go away!" Edward's mood was sharp. "I will manage on my own, thank you."

Lancaster stepped away again and whispered a report to the Archbishop.

"The king seems in ill humor."

Spurred to action, Edward grew red in the face with effort. Philippa tried desperately to hold back a laugh.

"You snigger at me?!" he demanded, offended now in embarrassment.

"I beg pardon, my lord, but you endeavor so earnestly. It makes your face rosy."

"Do you not desire me to complete my husband's duty? You tire of England and wish to return to your parents' keeping?!"

She touched his face to calm him, "No, royal husband, my wish is that you bear my heart, for I give it gladly, and my only desire is that—" she whispered softly in his ear, "you fill me with love's majesty."

Edward laughed, at last forgetting his great effort, now just looking into her eyes.

Philippa let out a small gasp of surprise as she felt a change. "My lord! You warm!"

The attendant lords exchanged attentive glances, as there seemed to be some rumbling around under the sheets. Philippa let out a small cry of pain and other sensation, holding her breath for a moment and arching her back.

"My lord does fill me," she whispered again.

The Archbishop stepped quickly to the side of the bed to lift the cover to peak underneath. Lancaster joined at his side and peered under as well. Mortimer also looked with appraisal.

"The marriage is consummate," Lancaster announced to the waiting host.

The Archbishop reached under the covers to pull out a kerchief stained with first blood and held it up for the audience to verify the virgin consummation.

One of the foreign emissaries stepped close to look under the sheets as well, but Edward jerked the blanket down.

"Now, will you leave us!"

Lancaster acted the cattle herd as the crowd was not swift enough in departure. "All out. Leave the king to his duties." A couple of prelates lagged behind with the Archbishop.

"Make haste!" Edward shouted.

The Archbishop was slightly offended. "His Grace is ill tempered today."

As the last witness left the chamber, Richard closed each entrance door and nodded to Edward with a wink, departing with the last, leaving them alone. Edward and Philippa both broke into laughter, looking into one another's eyes. The audience and indeed the world had vanished and it was only the two of them together. Edward kissed her and the task at hand seemed to come now with ease and pleasurable sensation as she wrapped her legs around him underneath the sheets.

Soon, even lowly servants and wards about the palace could testify that the marriage was sealed, if judged by the vocal sounds emanating from the privy chambers.

As the attendant lords made their way to other halls, heading for the waiting food and drink, Mortimer and Isabella paused, that they might not be heard. Isabella had many conflicting feelings about her son fulfilling his duty not far from them. He was settled in marriage as a mother would hope for a son, but she would no longer be the first in his mind for solace and counsel.

"What does Mortimer think of the young bride who now wears my crown on her golden head?" she teased.

"You know my feelings. We were agreed." He would not return to the long argument that he had hoped for an alliance with his own family.

"When Mortimer viewed the maid's form, did his eye not blanch with delight?" she continued her tease, but turning to bite of jealousy. "Is my woman's shape so quickly aged he must look on another to be reminded?" This had also become a familiar refrain from her as the marriage had drawn closer.

"I need no other," he assured her. To calm her, he pressed her into a nook, barely out of public view, and reached a hand underneath the fold of her outer garment to give her attention, but they were interrupted.

"Lady Cousin, a word, I am distraught—" It was Lancaster who stood apart in the hall, not commenting on their intimacy, which he knew well.

"Then speak your mind," Isabella said as they divided apart, straightening her gown with deliberate attention.

"I have been named Protector of our former King's Person, yet when I go to Berkeley to inquire of his well-being, I am kept from him by warders who tell me his state of health will not support visitors. When I complain that such a state is my legal concern, I am told it is by your order he is kept secluded."

Mortimer stepped forward between them. "It should not concern you, Lancaster. His care is well attended."

"His care is my duty." Lancaster stepped closer to Mortimer so that he might see into his eyes. His vision had been dimming around the edges as age advanced, and he liked to read men's faces at close range. "If I may not see him, I must conclude some injustice may be done, and if I believe it so, I must bring it to the King and the Council." He looked between them for an understanding of his concern. "I know my lady holds small love for her husband, but I beg you to not let heat lead to rash act. There already grows a murmur of discontent among the people."

"I thank you for your caution, Cousin, but my husband is in good hands," was Isabella's simple and final reply.

Mortimer faced Lancaster with a dark smile, "It would be best old Lancaster looked to his own health. As time wears on his years."

He took the threat as it was meant. "As it does on us all, Lord Mortimer. On us all." He bowed in courtesy and left them.

Isabella's temper rose at the encounter and she recalled Edward's pleading to be reunited with the former king, removed now from his reach. "My son also pines to forgive his father."

Mortimer reminded her that the gaolers at Berkeley were doing their best to weaken the former king in his cell chamber, if they would be rid of him, but he would not be soon gone without some firmer action.

"Je demander ma justice!" the lady seethed.

2

A great tournament was held at Windsor on the great open fields bounded by the river where the wedding of King and Queen Consort would be honored. Horses galloped with steaming breath and pounding hooves on the snow covered ground. Two knights charged in the lists, one dark and the other in silver armor with the three lions of the Plantagenet. Edward was skilled at the lance, and his crown-point struck sharply on the other's shield, the wood shaft shattering with a crack, but sending the challenging knight crashing to the earth.

As the crowds gathered along the tournament battleground cheered, Edward spun his horse and raised his visor to shout with a lusty, hormonal voice at his victory. He was now a man of seventeen at arms, but yet still a boy in legal decree, his full right as king held from him by the council.

Philippa stood on the viewing platform with the other court ladies, all bundled in winter coats. She also cheered proudly with them.

Edward rode to the fallen knight and lowered his broken lance. The beaten knight untied a lady's kerchief from the lance hook of his breastplate and draped it on the king's lance. Edward, with Philippa's garter tied to his own breastplate, rode to the scaffold and presented the kerchief to her. With a curtsy, she handed it to the Lady who had given it to the fallen knight. The ladies laughed as Edward made his horse to bow.

Two young knights rode up and saluted Philippa from their saddles. She made a great show of choosing and finally lay a kerchief on the tip of one knight's lance, that he might be the queen's champion.

They spun and charged off to battle. Edward enjoyed their exuberance as much as Philippa. He suddenly removed his helmet and climbed from his horse onto the scaffold. The ladies shrieked and laughed as he made way among them to take his wife in his gauntleted arms to kiss her.

"Isn't this glorious?!" he said, looking around at the festive flags and crowds of his people as he imagined since his youngest days of hearing the stories.

"It is much like Camelot must have been and you are my Guinevere. God, I feel today like justice and honor might live forever!"

"You are wonderful on horse," she praised, feeling his passion for the ideals of chivalry.

"If only my father might be here," he said with a rising pang. "I so wanted him at our wedding."

"Does your mother have such power over you?" Philippa asked. She had seen the pull her mother-by-law held over her husband. "Can you not be a dutiful son and your own man as well?"

Edward looked to his mother. She was with Mortimer among the familiar barons who now seemed to always surround them on official occasions, their council allies and Mortimer's sons. Yet, Isabella was not interested in their conversations but instead watched with envious eyes the new young and beautiful queen consort, receiving the attention of the crowds which used to be hers.

"Yes, by God! Let her take it how she may. I will go to him." Edward was resolved that he would defy his mother's wishes that he not see his father, but he was still cautious not to challenge her in the open unless his attention be seen as a wish to pardon his father, which she would not brook.

"Soon," he said, with a sad feeling at the weakness he felt to challenge her. He did not know that it was already too late. A monstrous plan for the deposed Caernarfon had already been put into motion.

Berkeley Castle had been in the hands of the same family since Robert Fitzharding was first granted the barony of Berkeley by Henry Plantagenet while the future king was still the Duke of Aquitaine. Fitzharding was not a soldier or noble like many of the barons who supported Henry, but a wealthy merchant from the port city of Bristol who financed Henry's campaign to advance to the throne of England against King Stephen, beginning the Plantagenet dynasty. Fitzharding had built a strong keep on the westernmost land bordering the Severn River, which divided England and Wales, where it served as one of the mighty fortresses which formed a defense against the Welsh. The castle was now held by Thomas, the Third Baron of Berkeley, who had maintained his ancestor's wealth and had allied himself with Mortimer through marriage to his eldest daughter.

The former king, Edward Caernarfon, had been removed from Lancaster's protection at Kenilworth and handed to Thomas Berkeley for keeping under Mortimer's influence in joint custody with John, Baron of Maltravers. Maltravers had been an ally of Lancaster in former days. It was to his care that Lancaster had agreed when it was proposed he be removed from Kenilworth. This would prove to be a fatal choice.

The floor of the corridor of the old Norman keep at Berkeley was damp with dew and strewn with rotting slaughtered chickens and crawling with rats feeding on the carrion. Fresh apartments for the family had been constructed for comfort inside new walls connected to the former stronghold, now kept for storage of arms. The Baron Thomas had removed to his other northern holding lands on warning that he should not be at Berkeley. Flies buzzed in a dreadful stench as heavy footsteps and jangling keys were heard outside the former king's cell.

Edward Caernarfon sat on a hay mat on the stone floor of the chamber, ringed with dead animals crawling with vermin, intended to give him disease. The bones and waste of the meager food he had been given lay unremoved, but only as far from him as he might push with his foot. The gloomy chamber was neither light nor dark as the small windows had been boarded and smeared with excrement. The chamber turned prison cell was filthy and fetid. He wore only a tattered shirt and ate from a bowl of maggot-ridden mush.

The apartment had once been comfortable enough when he was first brought there and visited by lords of the council, with a bed and writing desk where he could be viewed through a small opening where a tapestry of a royal hunt had been hung upon the wall. He had spent his time then writing poems and pleading letters to his son. But the letters were never delivered and the council representative's visits denied on one excuse or another, until the furniture had been removed and the chamber turned to foulness.

He was startled by the sound of the keys turned in the heavy lock. "Edward, my son? You've come at last?" he called out in raised hope.

The heavy door was thrown open with a thud against the wall. Maltravers and his other appointed guardian, Sir Thomas Gourney, entered with dark intent.

"What, still not dead, thou king of muck?" Gourney mocked him. "The carrion has not made you sick enough?"

"Is my boy come to visit me today?" he asked in hope. His body, kept in health by his years of swimming and activity, had proven strong against all attempts to bring him down by illness, but his mind had been weakened in solitude and torment.

Gourney smiled at him, "You will have visitors aplenty to see you crowned in your new kingdom." It was clear that a plan to seal his fate had been decided.

Several burly men rushed in. Caernarfon saw what was to come and scrambled to get away, but three of the men grabbed him. Gourney pulled some straw from the mat and bent them into a crown-like ring to place on his head.

"Your crown, Your Grace. And here is your scepter."

Another man entered carrying a fire hearth poker, glowing red hot. Caernarfon struggled against the strong arms holding him.

"No! No!" he cried out.

His struggles were so violent, it took six men to throw him face down on the floor while two others grabbed the wooden table and upended it onto his back, holding him down so that his naked legs protruded from underneath.

Maltravers produced a metal pouring horn with a hole big enough for the glowing poker to pass through. "Our masters, Bishop Orleton, Lord Mortimer, and your loving Queen bid us leave no mark upon the body. So, let this be the last foul organ to enter where others have defiled."

As they brought the horn and glowing poker near, Edward Caernarfon cried out in last tearful anguish. "Why does my son not visit me?!"

They stuffed his mouth with a fetid, soiled rag to muffle his screams, but still, many who came near the castle could hear the horrid cries from within.

3

Far from the dark deeds of Gloucester, Edward and Philippa sat side by side on their thrones in the great hall of Westminster, underneath the banner of the three lions as the sun's rays filtered through the high colored-glass windows, casting dancing dust mites in rainbow glow as a line of petitioners, nobles that wished their sons knighted and commoners who hoped to have some grievous wrong righted that only the king and not his justice courts could address, waited for their moment with the King and his bride Queen.

A young couple with no grievance at all had brought their newborn babe to be blessed. It was a small matter, but hope for a new rise of joy had brought them. Edward made the cross with his thumb on the baby's forehead. Philippa rose from her chair to kiss the infant. The child's parents beamed with pride and Edward reached to take Philippa's hand, in their own happiness.

Among the support columns of the hall, Mortimer leaned himself against the wall, so that he might not be noticed as he watched the blissful young lovers like a falcon studying his prey. His black eye fell especially on Philippa's sweet smile, she who now sat in the place he had hoped would be the place of his family. Yet, even as he watched, the new babe in arms presented to them, a fresh plan came into his mind.

The newly blessed child suddenly started to wail, as if pricked by some unseen needle, and its parents made their apology before they were ushered away. As they were guided from the hall with profuse apologies, Richard entered from the vestibule, hurrying through the doors. He dreaded telling the news he had brought. He pulled Edward from the line of subjects and whispered in his ear.

Philippa saw her husband distracted and watched as he started painfully. He quickly pushed himself from the great throne of his office and strode across the hall, ignoring the waiting host, running out from the place.

Philippa asked Richard what had happened to affect him so.

"His father is dead."

Edward hurried to his mother's apartments, striding down the hall, eyes reddening, but his long steps were not enough and he ran to his mother's chamber door.

"Mother!" he called, for he was still a boy.

He threw open the door of his mother's solar to find Isabella sitting on her stool, sewing with needle point, surrounded by her French serving maids.

"Maman! Mon pere est morte!" he cried in anguish.

Isabella simply nodded as if it were a matter of common knowledge. "Je suis informer. It is said that he—" she delighted in pronouncing the common English phrase "took a chill. I am told he was ill for some time."

"And that is all you care to know?!"

"I am satisfied. Regardez—!" She held up what she had been sewing, a tunic with two panels of the Three Lions of the Plantagenet of England on a field of red combined with two panels of the Capet Fleur-Des-Lis of France on blue. "For when the crown of my husband and the crown of my father will be joined together on the head of my son."

"Mother!?" he blurted with little understanding of the depth of her hatred. "Your husband is dead, your father too, and you care only for their crowns?!"

"It is as much care as they gave to me," she explained with calm and cold patience. "My father traded his only daughter to the foreign English king as an offering for peace, and when I was deserted by my husband, he also turned away from my tears."

"And did we not sell my baby sister, and a crown for thirty-thousand gold marks!" Edward cried, recalling the Scottish settlement, in which he had signed away his sovereign rights. "Who will soothe her tears among strangers in far Scotsland? And the tears of my grandfather who must weep in his tomb."

Isabella hesitated a moment, in a dark place, but let it pass. Scotland had been a heavy price to pay for the loyalties which had brought down her husband, but perhaps it was not gone forever. It was to France she now turned.

The line of direct Capetians to wear the French crown was at an end. John I, who had become king as a newborn infant upon the death of Isabella's eldest brother, Louis X, had died after only five days and the French throne had succeeded in dispute to Isabella's next oldest brother, Philip V. The passing of the succession however was contested by Louis' eldest daughter, Joan, who claimed she would be next in line. To secure his hold on the crown, Philip had invoked the ancient Salic Law of the old Frankish kings, which only allowed for titles, lands and property to pass to the male heir, and the female held no right to succession. It was Isabella's intent to argue that even though the crown could not pass to her, as Phillip IV's eldest surviving child, the crown of France, rather than to her, should pass in most direct line to her eldest male progeny, Edward.

"My father is dead, as is my brother who took his place. You are next in line through me and I will see the two kingdoms joined in you. This is my dream." She offered her arms to embrace him, but he held back. He had lived with this dream of hers, and he believed the crowns of the two great kingdoms of the world should be joined, but he was not of such a single mind as his mother.

She asked him what was wrong, "Qu'est-ce qui ne va pas?" Mother and son could not have been farther distant than at that moment.

"My father never wronged me. Why did you make me forsake him?!"

"You are King. I make you do nothing." She was flippant.

"I am not King! You let me play!" He knew well his true place in the game. "You, and Mortimer, who habits your husband's bed! You set the stage and give me toys!"

"You will not speak so of gentle Mortimer. Ours is honorable friendship." The lie had been bared to all. Even now, the once praised wife of the former king who had raised an army to set her son on the throne was called among some "Shewolf of France".

"Honorable!? Honorable?" The word even seemed to catch in his throat. "Even Philippa has heard the foul gossip from scullery maids. It passes from lip to lip."

"Do you now take her counsel against me? My bed is not my child's province, nor his wife's." Isabella tried to turn from listening.

"It is the King's province when his mother is called whore in the streets!"

She slapped him. A king is still a son, and he was sorry he had said it to her face, but her reply was even more harsh, and telling of her own rising jealousies.

"It would be the wiser for the boy king to look to his own consort's bed lest it be another name whispered in the street—Phil-ip-pah!"

The great hall had been cleared of petitioners as the message of the former king's death had been passed amongst the court. Philippa had stayed to put on a brave show for the common subjects, but now retired to find her husband to console him. Mortimer blocked her path. They were near alone in the great hall.

"Sad news, I hear." Mortimer offered condolence, but she suspected he did not mean it. She had as yet no reason to dislike Mortimer. They had little chance for discourse in private until now.

"My husband intended to be reunited with his father. I only hope I may console him. Pardon." She curtsied to him, even though her station was above his, as she wished to give him all courtesy and not cause an ill feeling between them. She started to leave again, but Mortimer again stepped in her path. He, in turn, held her station as nothing at all.

"You have wisdom for a lady of such tender years, and a good heart for concern of your husband. He can be counted lucky."

"You are kind to me, Lord Mortimer. I understand you had hoped for a daughter of your own to have received my blessing."

"What parent does not wish the best for his children?" he smiled with a casual and studied shrug of his heavy shoulders. "I only hope now, you and I may become as close as blood relation—despite the chasm between our years."

He was soon to be fifty in years and she was sixteen, but this did not seem to matter to him as his age had not bent him in the least. He was still fit and vital, and though forward, she was not unflattered.

"Indeed, my lord, as I wish to be on pleasant term with all my husband's court, I will place no barrier beyond that which my office requires."

He bowed to her diplomacy, taking her hand to kiss it. "Your Grace is well deserved."

It was at this moment that Edward had returned to find her. He entered the hall just in time to see them together. He eased behind a pillar as Mortimer whispered something in Philippa's ear, making her smile. Mortimer bowed and departed. Philippa was escorted by attendants to the palace residence.

Just returned from his mother, with her own poisons fresh in his mind, Edward had waited until his wife was alone in a hall as she made her way to the family apartments, where he would confront her.

"What do you discuss so merrily with Mortimer?" he asked, with only a thin veil of feigned disinterest.

"Only court matters, husband." She was surprised at his sudden change in mood from the pain of his father's loss she had last seen in him. "He has a ready wit."

"Take care his wit does not make you unwise."

Philippa laughed sweetly at her husband's obvious jealousy. It was a sharp shift, but she took it as his eager care for her. She turned to the sparring which came naturally to her and had led them to the marriage vow.

"Is it so soon after our wedding, you already suspect me with one so ancient?" She thought she might give as much wit as she had received from him. "If you wish me to wear the iron belt of chaste, bid me and I will gird it gladly, and you possess the only key."

She could see he was yet still in pain, and did not want any concern for her loyalty to compound it more. She took his hand and held it to her breast. "My love does not yet fail me. See, feel my pulsing heart. Does it not beat thy name? Ed-ward— Ed-ward—Ed-ward."

His sudden jealousy faded like a passing cloud, and he kissed her, spinning her in a dance. Court pages, going about their duties, tried not to pay any notice. Edward pulled Philippa behind a tapestry where they could kiss and nuzzle in private, with the aspect for any who might pass of a lump with protruding feet behind the cloth.

Close-wrapped in the woven cloth, Edward kissed her and held her face. He whispered to her, "Forgive my temper. It is only because I love you. And I have to be wary of who I count my friends."

"Count me as your dearest friend. I only wish I could take some of your grief. I see it in your eyes."

He was troubled and confessed it. "My mother is satisfied in the natural way of my father's death—but I am not. I will have an investigation. And let the truth settle where it might. Even if on witty Mortimer."

"What if the truth points in your mother's direction?" was her question, which did trouble him.

~~~

CHAPTER SEVEN

1

12th day of May, 1329

The Castle Pontefract of the Lancasters was a strong and feared fortress in the west of York. An ancient structure had stood on the spot of buried dead from the times of the Celtic druids, and its mighty walls, wrapping around a hill in the forests, served as guardian of the road from York to the western coast. It was here that Thomas, Earl of Lancaster, had been condemned for treason by Edward Caernarfon, and many of his followers executed, hung and quartered. Thomas had insisted he only served the crown against the king's rising favorites, and paid with his life. Now, Henry of Lancaster gathered the remaining of those loyal to him and Caernarfon's son, Edward.

Lancaster had been at the side of Mortimer in defense of his brother and in service of the queen against those same favorites but had seen Mortimer take their place. He had advocated abdication and accepted protection of the former king at Kenilworth, but Caernarfon had been wrested from his care and was now dead, with whispers of a foul end.

Lancaster's health had sapped his vitality, his eyes failing and his bowels now a constant torment, so he gathered a council in his privy chamber and strained on a pot with painful constipation.

"I have had my fill of this Mortimer," he groaned while loyal lords of the highest rank waited on him. "He presses the Council to name him Earl of The March for the lands he has gained by false accusation against good men. I would be rid of him, but he is as stuck in me as yesterday's lunch."

All those attending were of close relation to the boy king, or the queen consort. Among them, Edmund, Earl of Kent, was the highest of rank in the country next to his nephew the king, Sir Henry, Lord Beaumont, who had fought at Caernarfon's side at Bannockburn, and Sir Robert Holland, Lord of Liverpool and Secretary to Thomas Lancaster, whose lands had been taken by the Despensers for his part against Caernarfon, and now restored.

"'Tis the Frenchwoman he bellies with who hands him unwarranted honors!" Holland bellowed.

"This is a change of heart, Holland. You would have gladly bellied with the beautiful lady yourself not a year ago. And she your relation."

Holland flicked his thumbnail off his tooth in derision. "I'd sooner bed a black widow than the shewolf."

"I had feared my nephew was blinded by mother's love," Edmund mused, "but this investigation of my brother's death is a hopeful sign. I am convinced it is murder."

"The investigation comes too late. Caernarfon's warders are all fled to France, taking with them any chance of truth." Lancaster let out a huge groan with attendant sputters. "No, this black Mortimer must be denounced in Parliament and to the King. I will ride to court with our list of grievances to set before Edward. May open his eyes."

"I'll with you to have my say," said Holland.

The old Earl Lancaster rose from the pot as his body servant in long-standing duty handed him the wiping towel. He took a look as the product, sanguine at the state of his health.

"Each day, more blood flows than honorable wasting."

2

Lancaster rode from his strong keep of Pontefract with Holland and an attending retinue of fourteen men, among them Henry of Beaumont, Thomas Wake, Thomas Rosselin and David de Strathbogie, son-in-law of Beaumont. They were unarmed for a diplomatic call upon the king at Windsor, approaching the ward gate from the Thames bank in casual column, when they were met by Mortimer, who rode from the trees before the gates to block the road. Lancaster could not see who the dark figure was with his failing eyes. He had to ask Holland to identify him.

"It is the Marcher who beds the wolf queen," Holland whispered.

"Then our purpose has been betrayed," Lancaster replied.

"No further," Mortimer challenged from astride his horse, sword at his side.

"I will see the King," Lancaster demanded.

"If you maintain any business with the King, dispense it with me."

"I will see the King or see you in hell. My eyes would not have me see you in the other place."

"Let it be wherever you wish." Mortimer raised an arm and suddenly twenty armored horsemen wearing the arms coat of Mortimer's Unicorn rode from the trees to attack. Lancaster's men were outnumbered, some of them only armed with daggers. Many quickly fell. With his position hopeless against odds, Lancaster turned his horse.

Holland turned with him to guard his retreat. He called back to Mortimer.

"We'll see you and your French harlot's heads on London bridge!"

Mortimer charged after Lancaster, but Holland kept his horse between them. Unable to reach

Lancaster, Mortimer swung his sword at Holland, cleaving through his neck.

As Holland's headless body tumbled from the horse, Lancaster escaped down the road with the few others left.

Isabella was startled when the door to her chamber opened without a knock. It was Mortimer who entered. He had a satisfied smile on his face.

"I've a present," he said.

"Let me see."

Mortimer stepped to the table which held her sewing tools and set upon it the severed head of Robert Holland.

"A knight who will not again dishonor your name."

Isabella's servant girls gasped in horror, but Isabella only looked at the head curiously. She dismissed her maids with a wave of her hand, and they quickly ran from the chamber.

"I know this head," Isabella said, recognizing "Sir Robert Holland. He was once a friend to me."

"A friend no more. He came with Lancaster to denounce you." Mortimer slapped a parchment on the table beside the bloody head. "A list of charges against us they were intent on delivering to the boy."

Isabella looked over the document, rising to quick rage. "Do all now turn against Isabel? She delivers to them a country and such is her reward? This

Lancaster would still be rotting in France if Isabel did not stir him to action! I will not be scorned!" She looked to the gruesome object on the table dripping blood.

"I will see him severed from his head as well as his lands for this!" She stared at the grim visage of Holland. She played her fingers in the sticky long hair as if he were an old lover alive. Then, a sudden mood shift to hurt and doubt.

"These men once sung her praise, yet now they revile Isabel. She is abandoned by all, but her son and her clever Mortimer." She touched his face. "You will never forsake me?"

"Never," he said and kissed her while the severed head looked on in silent witness.

3

In the hall of Windsor, Edward perched on the arm of his throne while Richard sat on a stool opposite with a round backgammon board set between them, but they were more involved in hushed discussion than play. Philippa stood by Edward, rubbing his back gently as he slapped his game pieces around the board. He was distracted by warring thoughts in his mind.

"I am blocked at every turn, Richard! My judicial inquiry meets with silence. My father's body has not been found for examination. But I have heard such horrible whispers. If I took them for any but morbid gossip, I might go mad."

The story of screams from the cell of Caernarfon at Berkeley had been passed among the common folk of Gloucester, heard by the servants and keepers of the household, and spread from court to court. The story of the horn was said by some to be a mean joke started by enemies of the former king, or enemies of the wolf queen, as his wife was increasingly named. Edward did not want to believe the stories and had decreed a commission to investigate the truth or falsehood, but any who may have been present had all fled away, to France it was suspected.

"I think I am halfway there," he laughed sadly. "I see conspiracies all around me. If only for something to act on!" He slapped a piece on the game board in his frustration.

It was in this mood when his mother rushed into the hall with Mortimer close on her heel. He was disturbed by her seeming emotion.

"Edward!" she cried. She was distraught, and on the verge of tears, not quite sobbing. She pulled at her kerchief in agitation.

"Maman, what is wrong?" he rose to meet her, concerned.

"We are betrayed! Lancaster has led men-at-arms to murder us in our own house. Only Mortimer's retainers were able to turn them back from our gate."

162

"My small party was set on by fifty of Lancaster's men. His claim is that you sit unlawfully on your father's throne. He threatens to return with an army of six hundred." Mortimer's story was mostly false, but Edward was quick to accept it.

"Does everyone plot against me!?" Furious, he paced with angered frustration. In such a mood, he often would walk from one point to another and back again as if in a cage.

"Are these barons so jealous of my crown! They think me such a boy, I cannot defend my right?" He had been among them when the lords who once bent a knee to his father turned to remove the scepter from his hand, and now had killed him. He had listened to his mother's complaints that the barons would try to advance beyond upon the words of the Great Charter signed by John to remove the crown from the one anointed by God's will to disperse ruling power among themselves, and here seemed such an example.

"Chastise them." Mortimer urged. "Let me ride against Lancaster and put down this rebellion."

Lancaster's brother had led the rebellion of the Barons against his father, and Lancaster now seemed, if these events were true, to be following in the same path. Edward had believed in his honor and loyalty, but if he were now betrayed by one so close, it was a powerful sting. If those who had been sworn to him deserted him, and it was seen that he was a weak king, still just a boy, he would be cast from his place like his father before.

"I cannot let it stand," he said. "I'll ride with you. Lancaster will state his case plainly to my face." Edward left the hall in a storm of intent to action. Mortimer followed him.

Philippa was left with the Queen Mother, worried for her state of mind, believing she was the same woman who had consoled her tears when she was a child.

"Vous voudrais accompagne, Maman Isabel?" she tried to offer comfort, but Isabella's tears quickly dried and she had nothing to say to the girl who now held her place. She gathered her skirts and swept from the hall after her son and Mortimer.

"My husband is quick to heat." Philippa turned to Richard for his counsel.

"Too quick I fear." He knew the king well, but had less commerce with his wife. "Do you have some disagreement with the Queen?"

"We do not speak, save for courteous greeting. And sometimes not even that," she said, saddened at the question. "Yet when I was small, I was fond of her visits to my mother." Then, she smiled secretively, letting Richard into her confidence. "Perhaps we will be friends again when I gift my husband with child."

Richard studied her secretive expression curiously, and she broke into a glowing smile.

"I have not been able to keep break-fast in my stomach for two days. I beg you, don't tell Edward until he returns. I would not have his safety distracted by worries for me."

"Our secret, then."

4

Edward rode at the head of a column of mounted men-at-arms across the stony fields of Lancashire to Pontefract. There were a few wearing the king's royal colors, but the larger number wore Mortimer's black, unicorn coat. Riding at Mortimer's side were his sons Henry and William, and with them two powerful knights, Sir Hugh Terplington and huge Sir John of Monmouth, a massive mountain in armor. Villeins scrambled from the path of the army as they trampled the fields.

A small company of knights with Beaumont at their head blocked the road leading to the castle, holding a white banner. Edward signaled his column with his raised hand.

"Hold! They fly the flag of truce," the young king ordered, but Mortimer had other designs. Terplington and Monmouth rode forward at the charge with the rest of Mortimer's cadre to the attack, while the king's host held their ground in confusion.

"Hold I say! Hold your ranks! Your King commands!" Edward shouted.

Mortimer's loyal force ignored him and soon overwhelmed Beaumont's men.

Mortimer held his horse at the king's side. "I fear they are too thrilled in Your Grace's service."

Edward could only watch from across the plain as the melee turned to a field of blood. Terplington struck Beaumont from his horse to the ground. When Beaumont fell, being chief among them, the rest of the company laid down their swords.

Edward rode among the hacked and wounded of Beaumont's men to where Beaumont struggled to rise on one arm, bleeding from a gaping sword wound. He had been at Edward's side in the crossing from France.

Edward dismounted and knelt, offering his hand, but Beaumont refused it.

"We thought you chivalrous and just, young king," Beaumont said to him, "but today brings dishonor when you ride with this band of thieves."

"I only respond to men-at-arms my uncle has raised," Edward replied.

"Lancaster has no complaint against you, Sire, only with the evil-eyed rascal who holds sway over you." Beaumont looked to Mortimer, holding his horse beyond. "If you would save England, my lord, let the closing of my eyes open yours." And so, he died.

"On to Castle Pontefract!" Mortimer commanded.

Edward stood to challenge him. "No!"

"Edward, this greedy peer has made treason." Mortimer was intent on his path. "His head should be forfeit with his lands."

"I have seen no proof of treason, only a hasty act of pride." Edward stood on his own against the lord who had taken the place of his father. "He will be held to account by justice of the Council. But no harm shall befall my uncle, without trial, on my honor."

Mortimer steamed at the challenge, on the verge of riding on, but Edward turned to the force, standing as tall as he could.

"Any man who crosses the draw of Pontefract without my leave will be counted traitor!" Edward ordered, looking up at the cold faces of Terplington and Monmouth on their horses with swords drawn. He felt so very vulnerable, standing off his horse. He could easily be cut down and claimed by deceit that it was at the hands of Lancaster's loyals. His own true loyal men were distant beyond those wearing Mortimer's coat. Mortimer rode his horse near to him, close enough to trample. His eyes met the young king's in deathly challenge.

"Very well. The justice of the Council—Your Grace." Mortimer at last turned his horse and rode to distance, followed by his men, leaving Edward standing alone.

Chaucer paused for breath, looking over his enthralled listeners. The shades of day were drawing dim now, but the story not yet done. He waited to see if they were still intent on understanding.

"Please, good sir, tell us whose will would be followed," asked the baker's son.

"Who would prevail?" pressed another.

Chaucer tousled the hair of a young eager listener. "Do not rush ahead for answer," he said, "for more darker shadows may arise than may be dispelled."

He continued his tale where he had left, yet spinning away the more tedious detail of politic and parliament, leaving only the essential matter for understanding.

5

The first bell had begun to ring at Windsor, in even-paced rhythm, not a somber tolling of death, but the joyous peel of life. Then, the bells at Westminster Palace took up the song, and the Tower, word first passing among the royal houses. Then in chapels about London, and Westminster Cathedral, until the great city was overcome with the clanging tones, and on to follow across the land, to cities great and the smallest of villages as the news spread, the Queen Consort Philippa was with child, portending a first born for the young king. It was most usual for the bells to ring with the certainty of a birth, but the common people were anxious for tidings of this young royal couple. The news of expectation would provide happy speculation and debate to lift them in hope from their hard lives. Would the royal offspring be boy or girl, prince or princess? And while joy visited the household, so did sorrow.

The late king, Caernarfon, was buried at St Peter's Abbey of Gloucester with a great procession of honor, three months after his passing, a wooden coffin born in pomp through the gates of the city. Edward, to honor him, had caused to be ordered an alabaster likeness of his father for a great tomb, with his head resting on a pillow, gently held by angels, even as rumors of the wicked means of his death spread. An investigation was begun, but all who could give testimony of the true events had fled. A proclamation demanding their return had been issued, but with a hopeless outcome.

Even as pilgrims began to flood through the gates of Gloucester to visit the miraculous likeness of the old king, with coins filling the coffers of the abbey and the city, stories spread like fire among the more hopeful, that the king was not dead at all, but had escaped his confining apartments of comfort at Berkeley to rise again as king, while others reveled in the more sinister manner of his murder, for gossip, like gold, seemed to gain value by the passing of it from one to the next.

The Ruling Council was firmly in Mortimer's grasp. Thomas of Lancaster was fined and stripped of his right as High Sheriff of Lancaster and forbidden to raise arms. He resigned from the council and was shortly followed in protest by the Earl of Kent and the last of the King's friends. Edward's vision of a new Camelot was fading as quickly as it had been born. Yet, still he held hope, even as he was invited to Kenilworth for what he was told would be a ceremony in honor of his father.

It seemed that peace had returned with the punishments of Lancaster and those who had joined him, as Edward arrived at Kenilworth with only a small company. The great castle of red brick where the crown of St Edward the Confessor had been wrested from Caernarfon and passed to his namesake son had been taken from Lancaster's diminished lands and given over to Mortimer's holding and the coat of black was present on men-at-arms in growing number.

Edward walked with his good friend, Richard, and a few close loyal knights, Montagu and Rokeby, through the long armory, lit with torches, the weapons of war now resting still in the stocks.

"It was here, in this chamber, I received the accolade of knighthood," Edward said, stopping to consider the long row of pikes held in reserve for battles which might rise in days or years ahead. "I vowed on the sword my rule would be for the good of my people and not the plunder of the land. Can that vow be so long ago?" he wondered. "With each passing, more lands go to Mortimer's adherents, with the stamp of the council in his grasp. Here we are where I began, with as little influence over my dominion's affairs as I had before kneeling."

Richard clapped a consoling hand on his shoulder. "There is time yet to keep your vow. Come on then, the function above already begins."

"I can only wonder what form of honor for my father Mortimer has in store. Some petty party, I suppose. Drink and wassail."

Edward had been invited by Mortimer to a celebration of Caernarfon's life and legacy, but what Mortimer had promised was far from what the young king was to be treated.

Edward and Richard entered the smoke-hazed, torch glowing upper hall, boisterously loud with men's voices. As Edward's eyes surveyed the room, he slowly burned with a rising rage. No ladies were present, but serving pages had been made to dress as ladies, with painted faces. In the center of the room was a round table, like King Arthur's. The chairs around it were occupied with Mortimer's friends, drinking and feasting on mutton and sweetbreads. They all wore

Mortimer's colors to show their allegiance. A banner with Mortimer's arms emblazoned, but with an Earl's coronet and the title "Earl of March" was suspended over the table from the rafters.

Mortimer rose from his throne-like chair at the far side of the table. The back of the chair was also embossed with the newly invented earldom's emblem.

"Cousin Edward, you arrive just in time. Join us in our solemn meal in honor of your departed sire. Take any seat, for like Arthur's table round you so much admire, all seats are equal to the others— nearly." Mortimer gestured to the knight next to him to get up. "Even come and sit beside me."

Edward burned at the mockery. Then he saw, lying in the middle of the table, the iron poker and pouring horn used to kill his father. With an agonized growl, Edward grasped the hilt of his sword and started to draw it, but Richard quickly pounced to hold him back. They were four against fifty.

"For Christ's mercy, Edward," he urged him to hold back. "We are witlessly outnumbered."

"If I die to avenge and honor my father, it will be a good death."

"Honor your father by living to be a just king, and think of the child your wife bears. I'll die at your side if you wish, but I'd much rather die in bed as an old man with a plump wife."

Edward finally released his sword hilt. He turned on his heel and stormed from the hall. Richard and Edward's loyals bowed to Mortimer and his men.

Montagu fixed Mortimer's dark, challenging glare. "My lord feels a twinge of indigestion at the sight of so over-rich a repast. Perhaps you will join us at our table where the company will be more even."

They exited, and Mortimer smiled with unadulterated joy as his loyals roared with laughter.

Edward and his company feared they might not be allowed out of the gates of Kenilworth, but Mortimer's designs had only risen to mockery, and he dare not raise a hand of violence, yet.

6

Returned once again to his familiar Windsor, Edward paced in frustration, ill-treating any furniture that might get in his way. Richard tried to counsel him, but he had little comfort to offer.

"If His Grace finds himself boxed in a room with no door, he has only himself to blame. Moving against Lancaster has only removed allies from your hand."

"I was deceived. And I swallowed the bait like a trout!" he raged.

Philippa came to the hall, hearing of her husband's return. Her belly was starting to show in her gown.

"Edward?" she said, hoping to gain his attention, but he was too lost in his own concerns.

He paced, oblivious to anything but his own mind. "This army of the west marcher counties follows Mortimer with no loyalty beyond their next meal. And the Council is a body of Mortimer's whims. They bend to name him Earl of the March with no precedent, save for his will, and I have no say, but putting my hand to it."

"Husband?" she asked again, hoping she might distract him from his troubles.

"You could withhold signing and not give consent." Richard suggested.

"And have it shown that I am not King, but only court jester?!" Edward knew he was in a trap. "If I have any hope for holding the loyalty of the lords, I must maintain at least the appearance of strength of command. Otherwise they would remove me like they did my father and shout all hail for the next unlucky bastard to take my place."

"My lord!" Philippa at last cried loud enough that he could not ignore her longer.

"What do you crave so, Philippa, it must interfere with my duty?"

"The babe tumbles. I thought you would like to feel his strength." She stepped nearer, presenting her pregnant stomach for him.

With an impatient sigh, he paused to touch her belly, not really expecting much, but as she placed his hand on the right spot, he brightened with pleasant shock. It was a sensation he had never known. There was a small feeling of movement there.

"I feel his heart!"

"Does it not pound?!" Philippa beamed with the joy of the moment. Edward touched her face tenderly. But his mind was still filled with politics.

"Parliament convenes in Nottingham in November." He turned from his pregnant lady to his counselor, fixing upon a thought. "I am soon eighteen and they cannot deny me much beyond, when it can no longer be argued that I am a callow boy. Until then, I must work what alliances I can in private."

"Who do you count among your friends in Parliament?"

"Montagu is still a fast friend, but he has small wealth. My uncle of Kent is the last ally I can count with strength of arms, if it comes to a matter of force."

"Then you must send word to your cheery uncle to harness his loyalty."

"Mortimer has eyes in every corner. I'm afraid any private communication sent by messenger will not remain private." He suddenly brightened with an idea. He slapped Richard on the shoulder and led him to the hall door, growing excited. "Organize a hunting party. A casual tour of the southern counties. And if we should happen to stop for rest at my uncle's house—who would say it's not natural?"

They left the hall, right past Philippa, feeling ignored like a piece of child-bearing furniture.

Mortimer arrived at Windsor from Wallingford, having followed Edward's retinue's return. He rode through the gate to find squires and grooms, cooks and chars busily packing wagons.

"What is this preparation?" he asked of a squire.

"The King goes hunting," was the reply.

Mortimer examined the wagons, going from one to the next, checking under the cloth covers to see what was intended. Finding nothing damning, he went on to the residence.

Isabella heard Mortimer from the window of her apartment. She urged her maids to finish powdering her.

"Vitte!"

She quickly looked in the reflecting glass, then hurried excitedly to the door, rushing to meet her returning lover.

Upon entering the hall chambers, Mortimer found Philippa rushing through the hall and she nearly ran into him, entering from out of doors.

"Lord Mortimer," she greeted him, but tried not to allow him to see her wet eyes, for she was in a much emotional state. She intended not to speak to him, but he held her.

"Where hurries the sweet lady who washes her face in salty rivers?" he said in that manner of smoothness and earnest concern of which he was well capable with the fairer sex, that had earned him a wealthy widowed wife and a place at the side of a spurned queen. "Give me the burden of your cares. It can't be the world's end."

Philippa could not hold back. "My husband goes traveling and leaves his unwanted wife behind. He forsakes me because I am fat with bearing and my skin blemishes!"

Mortimer smiled, well knowing this state of a woman's life, and how it might be used. "These signs of child should cause no tears. They only add a rosy hue to the cheeks of motherhood." He gently wiped her face with his strong hand. Her first instinct was to withdraw from him, but she felt calmed by the soft words she hoped to hear from another.

"My lord is again kind to me."

"It isn't kindness, but anger at a husband so cruel to ignore a lady who loves him."

It was at this moment of intimate congress that Isabella should enter near, but upon seeing Mortimer with the young Philippa, she paused out of sight, watching them as they spoke closely. And as she observed them, her lover's thrill turned black.

177

"Would the Queen allow me to feel the child?" Mortimer asked of Philippa, and without waiting for her answer, he rested his hand on her belly. She was unsure whether she should protest his familiarity, but she felt somehow soothed in her emotion by the attention she craved from another.

"You have gentle hands for a warrior accounted so fearsome," she praised him, hoping that they might at least be friends.

"You count my reputation too much." He cooed in a velvet tone. "I issue from a line of blood as rich as your husband's. My Normandy ancestor Hugh Mortimer fought at the right hand of William Conqueror and was as near in royal lineage. Should I not be as versed in courtly manner as any king?"

Philippa allowed herself a small flirt with the still virile lord who was near three times her years. "You are indeed well-suited to courting, my lord. Time has only given your face handsome etch."

"Now, my lady is kind."

Philippa's maid came looking for her mistress, shocked to find her with Mortimer. Lea curtsied to the lord and delivered her message.

"Lady, thy husband calls for you!"

"If he truly wants me, he can come himself. I am not his vassal. Go and tell him I am occupied," she told her and warmly demonstrated her independent will by taking Mortimer's arm to accompany her.

With a huff and familiar roll of her eyes at her mistress's present moods, which had been growing as her belly advanced, Lea bustled off to deliver the message, sure she would receive another from the king and be sent back again.

As her daughter-by-law warmly took Mortimer's arm, Isabella, from her private viewing place, seethed with fury. She was well familiar with his intimate manner with her. Seeing it applied to another made her spin on her heel and hurriedly return toward her chambers where she might vent her mood, out of the presence of any who might see her weakness.

"And where does the king travel, so it takes him away from his loving wife?" Mortimer asked, arriving at his object.

Philippa was uncertain if she should reveal too much, but felt it could not hurt to allow the main of what she had been told. "He goes hunting at his uncle's southern county."

Isabella stormed into her private chamber and slammed the heavy door with all the strength she held and let out an anguished cry which frightened her maids. They were well familiar with these raging states of their mistress, which she only expressed with no-one else to observe, and had suffered an increase with each passing year.

"Sortez!" she ordered.

They quickly exited the chamber, lest they might receive the brunt of her attention. Once they were gone, Isabella careened about the apartment in unleashed fury, throwing furniture aside, ripping at tapestries with her fingernails, and smashing vases that had been given as expensive gifts from foreign ambassadors to honor her.

When she flung her sewing tools from their table, left lying behind was a thread knife. She grabbed it up, then with both hands ripped open the bodice of her gown, uncovering her bare bosom. She dragged the knife tip across the top of her left breast in self-loathing.

"Repugnante!" she cried, "Repugnante!" At last, with her rage spent, she collapsed upon her cushions. As she sobbed softly among the shattered rubble of her chamber, she could hear the clatter of horses on the grounds beyond the leaded window panes and the voice of her son below.

All preparation for travel had been made, and Edward gathered his horse's reins in the courtyard, ready to ride out with his caravan. He paused to look about for Philippa. He expected her to see him away, but she was nowhere to be seen.

"Where is my wife? Does she not want to bless my parting? I would much like to touch her belly again and kiss her for a sweet memory." Edward turned to Richard, puzzled. "She has been very strange of late."

"Maybe the child. I've heard that women in her way behave more mysteriously than usual." Richard counseled, with as little experience as his master.

"It must be. Perhaps she will have it delivered by our return and all will be again as normal." He wondered if those many lords he had known who had wed ladies they had never met before the marriage arrangement, or who only had commerce with wives who lived in their far-off land holdings, confronted similar comportment.

"We can wait no more," he said at last with distracted impatience. He prepared to mount his stamping horse, but stopped as a woman's voice caught his ear. He turned to the gate expecting his love, but it was his mother rather than wife who emerged from the ward. Isabella hurried across the ground with all signs of her anguish gone.

"Edward!" she called to him. "You must not go!"

He paused with one foot in the stirrup, "Why not?"

"I have heard disturbing whispers," she said, touching his face as she commonly did when they were in private, for it annoyed him under the eyes of others.

"What whispers? Talk of ladies' dressing gowns?" He had come to find that his mother's interest in foreign intrigue and matters politic had in the past years begun to shrink from the grand stage to matters of dress and fashion, which more and more occupied her.

"Ladies' undressing." She made as to speak in private, yet well public enough that all around might overhear. "Your queen is inconstant."

Even he was surprised. "It is idle gossip! You will not say this to me!"

"I have witnessed it myself."

The sudden burn of emotion which had cause to afflict him when better reason should prevail, especially where his mother was concerned, rose in his throat. "Then, it is your mother's jealousy that makes you say it."

"It is my mother's love that makes me say it. There are harsher rumors still. I do not want to believe the child she bears belongs to another, but I fear the truth." Yet, Isabella well knew the strings of her son's heart that she might play like an instrument. "She is even now with the false father."

"No! It's a lie! I won't listen more." He angrily mounted his horse and turned the animal to ride, but he turned it back again in indecision, the thought gnawing at his mind, burning. He once more turned his horse to go, then, yet back again. The horse's hooves clattered on the cobblestones, as he turned it and turned again, like a performance at a faire. Finally, unable to stand it longer, he jumped from his horse and strode back toward the inner ward.

Edward went swiftly through the apartments and halls, throwing open any doors or tossing back any curtains, peering into the rooms, looking for Philippa. He finally came upon her in a solar in Mortimer's company. She was resting her arm upon his, and speaking in casual manner. Edward took this as the betrayal planted in his mind and grown with every curtain he had peered behind.

"Then, it is true! I am deceived!"

Philippa, still young, had yet to see the full flare of her husband's darker passions, ruled by his mother's influence. She allowed herself to enjoy his jealousy, taking it for the attention she craved from him. She challenged him defiantly. "Does my neglectful husband now blanch at the sight of his lady in the company of another?"

Yet, Edward's agitation had boiled to a rage which would blind his more discerning reason. He only saw what he imagined.

"Whore!" he charged her.

She was stunned by the ferocity of his condemnation. "My lord, you make overmuch of so small a thing in a neglected wife."

Edward spied an armament display on the wall and stumbled to it, grabbing a sword.

Mortimer rested a hand on his own sword hilt, ready for confrontation, but Edward leveled his sword at Philippa.

"I'll kill the damned thing, and you beside!"

"Edward?! What vexes you so?! What is it you think I have done?!" She did not know the rumor he had been told but only could see the pain in his eyes.

Edward held himself teetering on the edge. He loved her and had no desire to harm her, but his mind was filled with thoughts of the enemies who surrounded him, Mortimer chief among them, standing now, touching the one object he had counted as pure in his life, untainted by conspiracy. Finally, he dropped the sword, yet with an animal growl, grabbed Philippa by the hand and pulled toward their private apartments.

"What is wrong?!" she asked in tears, only knowing that he was so angry she could only hope to reason with his kindness. "What is my husband going to do?! If you would beat me, I only beg you beware the child!"

Edward pulled her with no further words to the door blocking her own private chamber. He wrenched open the door and swung her into the room, staring at her for a moment, unable to find the words to explain his rage, or afraid to say them, lest they sting her more deeply. He slammed the door closed again and threw the bolt, as if the heavy wood and lock would protect her from the evil world, and from his own darkness. Drained, he slumped to the stone floor outside the door, leaning against it.

Inside the chamber, Philippa stared at the barred door, eyes stinging red and confused. She could tell he was still outside the door, unmoving and unspeaking.

"Edward?!" she called to him through it. "Husband?! Tell me what I have done!"

She received no reply from him and hit at the heavy door with her small fist. With still no answer from him, she, too, sank to the floor, in loss and confusion at his harshness. She cried aloud, weeping, and calling his name again that he might hear her and answer.

"Edward?! Edward?!"

In the courtyard below the royal apartments, Isabella and the riding party could hear the emotional voices from the chambers above. Isabella, in particular, was satisfied with herself. Richard sadly dismounted from his horse with the rest of the traveling party, traveling no more, the ally seeking trip surely postponed.

Mortimer, too, listened with some satisfaction to the sounds of marital discord which could be heard throughout the halls. His plan had been to woo the young queen enough that he might make her a confidante from whom he could learn the king's private intents, but the display of the young man's unfettered passion seemed a better tool than even he could have devised. It was in this state of mind, a pair of hands covered his own eyes from behind. A moment's dread flickered, as if it was the jealous boy who had returned in stealth, but the moment's fear quickly passed as he knew the soft touch and the familiar scent.

"Isabella—" he cooed.

"I am surprised Mortimer still knows my name."

He turned to meet her challenging gaze. He knew he need manage her jealousy as well. "It would take the tolling of death's knell ere Mortimer forget Isabel's gentle ring."

"Oui." her mood was still biting, well-acquainted with his courtly diplomacy. "Mortimer is never short of the bee's honeyed words, yet he finds Isabel such a wilted old flower he suckles nectar at fresher blossom."

"Isabella. You are the only flower at which Mortimer bumbles." he pulled her close to him. She tried to resist him, but she could not.

"I only woo the girl to discover what private counsels her husband may give to her. The young Queen reveals your son intends to visit the Earl of Kent."

"I expect he is distracted." Philippa's unhappy crying could still be heard from the chambers above.

"So, we may take advantage." Mortimer proffered. "I hear Kent feels the guilt of Cain for his part in the fate of his brother."

Isabella studied him. "How is it, Mortimer's mind is never far from his plottings?" She read his intent, but felt her own care waning, "while Isabel grows tired of the game."

"It is age's wage," he replied, measuring his own time left to him. "I am not so easily distracted by youth's passions. Yet, I would wish that Isabella might also try to keep her eye on the target."

~~~

CHAPTER EIGHT

1

9th Day of January, 1330

Edmund Kent knelt at the confessional altar of his castle chapel in Dover. His old confessor had in recent time, gone to that other unseen plain to test how his prayer had been accepted at the doorstep of his Holy Lord, and a series of fellow brothers had risen to be considered to take his place. It was so that the King's uncle now had a hooded monk before him he did not know. Yet, as he crossed himself and prepared to pray, the monk halted him with a whisper.

"My Lord Kent, before I hear thy confession, I have confess of my own for your ears."

Edmund, always fascinated with the gossip which passed among the lower orders, halted himself to hear the latest. He preferred to hope that some very unholy mischief might be revealed.

"Speak freely, then," he said. "I fear my confession today may be much too dull for your entertainment. It's not been a great week for sinning."

Yet, the monk was not offering some modest offense but professed to hold a secret knowledge which would deeply disturb and excite the earl. "I have serious news, my lord. Your brother, Caernarfon, yet lives!"

"What?! How have you heard this?"

The monk drew closer, so as no other might hear. "I have come late to your household from the monastery at Wells. In my travels, I made a night's stop at Corfe Castle, where I observed with my own eyes the former king thought dead, feasting with some small company. Shocked I was, yet I inquired of a brother of my order and was told Caernarfon is held prisoner there in secret these many months."

"Christ's balls!" Edmund exclaimed at the news. "Do you swear this to be true?!"

"Lord! You risk damnation!" The monk cautioned the royal earl's renowned excitability. He crossed himself to seal his earnestness. "I do swear it."

Forgetting his confession altogether, Edmund bolted from the chapel, flinging the door open. Light flooded the cramped chamber, casting a garish beam on the monk. If this had been the case a moment before, the Earl Kent might have recognized the monk as a deacon to Bishop Orleton, arrived in disguise to deliver the intended bait. And it was well delivered, for the eager lord swallowed the hook.

2

Corfe was a singular keep on the windswept southern coast. It had stood strong against Viking assault and was one of the first castles on English shores to be fortified by stone by Henry I after his father's conquest of Harold. King John had such confidence in its strength he had kept his crown jewels within its walls.

Edmund's horse clomped restlessly on the wooden bridge of the lonely castle draw as its rider knocked on the closed door of the gate. He had come alone to Corfe, fearing that none should hear of his mission to uncover the plot which had been perpetrated to conceal the fallen former king. He had not even consulted his familiars of his intent. This was not the first of the rumors that Caernarfon met not his true end at Berkeley but had been secreted away, yet it was the first Edmund had heard of a sighting of his living brother. Some believed it, others did not. And for the sake of his love for his brother, he intended to determine fact or fiction for himself. After a long wait, a small viewing door in the larger door of the gate was opened and Sir John Deverill, the castellan of Corfe peered out at the mounted visitor.

"State your business."

"I would speak with Edward of Caernarfon," Edmund demanded.

"Who wishes to speak?" Deverill asked in return, unrevealing that he was fully expecting the earl's inquiry.

"His brother of Kent."

The portal closed again. Edmund waited impatiently for his answer, holding his uneasy horse. Then again, the portal opened and Deverill peered out.

"He will not see you."

"He will not—or cannot?" Edmund was incensed that a brother of his rank, though no longer king, should still be accorded his due privilege, and so must be held a prisoner.

"He sees no-one," was the reply

Edmund handed a parchment that he had caused to scribed should he find evidence of the truth of the monk's story. "Then give him this letter of my brother's love for him."

Deverill reached through the portal to take the letter.

"Will you see he gets it?"

"I will see it delivered to him it is intended," Deverill replied with an uncertain meaning, then slammed the port closed again, leaving Edmund of Kent alone, his horse's hooves clamping on the old wood of the keep's draw.

3

A two-wheeled covered wagon jostled along a rutted muddy road in the drizzling rain surrounded by King's Guards on horse. A royal caravan was on the move from the great castle of Windsor to the Plantagenet family's manor at Woodstock, in the forested marshes of the River Glynne.

Edward rode in somber silence alongside the wagon. When it bounced in a deep rut, a soft yelp came from inside the cloth cover.

With only Lea and two loyal maids attending her, Philippa rode in the jostling wagon on many cushions. A fur blanket covered her very big stomach, but the layers could not soften the jolting ruts of a road, or the unreasoned, to her, damning judgment of her beloved. She leaned on her arm, trying a new position, wiping her red eyes from crying.

"Why does my husband treat me so?!" she shouted through the cloth cover to Edward she knew was near outside. "You are so ready to trust the lies of others and believe me unfaithful who loves you so much?!" There was no answer, just the rattle of the wagon and snorts of Edward's horse. "If I am so clever in my deceiving, do you think an army of armed guards can keep me true? Then, who would guard me from my guards?!" Still no answer. "Will you not speak to me?!!"

Outside of the wagon, Edward rode on in silence. He could hear the pained pleading of his consort, but he dare not allow himself to answer her, for he feared that what he would say might only cause more discord. In truth, he searched his own heart, for he did not know entirely what he felt, believing himself so surrounded by schemes that he could put his trust in no one.

The royal summer manor at Woodstock was ancient and much less a fortress than other royal strongholds. There were no garrisons of soldiers billeted for war, nor court of lords, nor petitioners for the king's attention, and private for birthing away from the burdens and bustle of great castles. Its setting was within the wooded plains of the wool lands of Oxfordshire, near were the grey stones of this western land formed a contrast to the green overgrown meadows where stone fences divided the sheep of tenant farms. It was here at Woodstock Edward's great-great-grandfather, Henry II Plantagenet, the first lion of England, wooed his Rosamond, and caused the disaffection of his queen Eleanor and his sons, Richard and John. So, it was fitting that the love of a young king might here also be tested.

Out of doors, black clouds of a roiling summer storm crackled with brewing energy, while within the stony walls, a fire snapped in the hearth of the hall where Philippa rested on the cushions spread for her and Edward paced in his manner of a beast of prey caught within a cage, from one arch to another, and returning again. Their discourse was unsettled and continued in argument.

"You pace like the lion of England, but are you so ready to feast on the lamb of Hainaut?" Philippa's tears had dried, but her anguish was not salved, as she tried to reach his heart. "I would no sooner be unfaithful to you than give up my life!"

"I am surrounded by false enemies," he answered her, as if trying to convince himself of his own reasoning.

"And this is why you believe me false?"

"I will see the child as proof of what you swear."

"Then rip me open and have your proof!!" she cried. "You will not accept my word. Name the time and place I have committed this foul coupling."

So influenced by the whispers of his mother's accusations, Edward had counted the days and hours. "About the time I went to Lancaster. It was just a month after my return, I am informed my queen grows thick."

"You were so much in turmoil, I did not tell you because I wanted not to cause you more worry. Ask Richard. He will vouch my truth."

He had no answer.

"Or is it you think I couch with Richard as well? And any stiff knight or dog that crosses within my lustful grasp?"

"I will see the child," was his only reply, his mind set in a round of circling reason, which always returned to the same answer.

"Why will you not believe me?!" Philippa could only scream in pain at her failure to reach his heart. Then, the pain of her soul turned to the real pains of childbirth. She suddenly cried out with a gasp and clutched at her belly, falling to the floor.

Edward rushed to her, calling out, "Midwives!"

He held her in worry as the pain ripped through her, but from where it arose, he couldn't tell. He could only wait with her until they came to aid.

The lightning crackled, casting shards of brightness on the fields and manor keep as thunder boomed through the night. A pouring rain tumbled from the sky as Richard arrived by hurried horse. He had urgent news for his friend the king, which he bore with a heavy weight of time's press.

He found Edward in the hall, still pacing as he had for hours, not like an expectant father but more a trapped panther, bouncing off one wall and propelling himself to the other, again and again.

In the apartment chambers above, the midwives bustled in their duties around the queen consort, spread out on the bed, her skin covered in sweat and panting in pain. She bucked and writhed as the ladies tried to keep her still and moistened her forehead. There was little they could do as the labor progressed in agonizing pace. They had assisted difficult labors, but this was more than they had seen in recent memory in any which the mother survived.

The shrill stab of a shriek of Philippa's pain emanating from the bed chambers greeted Richard as he observed the king, and the cry chilled him.

"Edward?" he prodded the king gently with recognition of the voice, "the child comes?"

Edward hardly paid notice to Richard, standing by, as he examined his own soul for God's judgment. "My wife is punished. Yet, I don't know whether for her sin, or mine." He turned to Richard with anguish in his eyes, "What frightens me most— If she is free of guilt, then my sin is so much greater than any I accuse her of, and she is twice punished."

Richard felt for his anguish and could not wish him to suffer more, but he could no longer withhold his urgent news, "Edward— Your uncle Kent is arrested and charged with treason!"

"No!' he cried, wanting to push away the thought. "My uncle would not turn on me."

"By some means, he came to believe your father to be alive and kept at Corfe. He gave a letter offering help to his brother. This has been made as treason against you by familiars of the Lord of Corfe. In your absence at court on these family matters of your wife, Mortimer and your mother took it to the council and hold hasty trial in Winchester. If you hope to intercede, scribe a writ for me to carry. I fear they have already fixed a sentence."

Edward listened and considered what he must do. "No, they could burn the paper, or claim it was delayed. I must go myself. Prepare horses—"

At that moment, Philippa shrieked again and Lea scurried into the room with blood on her hands.

"My lord, the infant comes sideways!" she cried.

Edward left Richard in the midst of instruction and fearfully rushed toward the chambers.

Edward threw the door aside to enter Philippa's birth chamber, but one of the midwives turned to see him.

"Your Grace, you mustn't come here! This is woman's place."

Edward ignored her and stepped closer past the chubby hips of the midwife to view Philippa, looking on her sweat drenched and pain contorted face. Her eyes caught him.

"My loving husband has come for his proof?!" she cried in gasping breath. "Yet, if he needs proof of his wife's love—he proves he loves her not!!"

She convulsed with a bolt of pain as a bolt of lightning cracked outside the lead-pained window, casting her form in ghostly white.

"Your mother has poisoned you against me!" Whether the pain of the breach or his unjust suspicion was the greater, could not be distinguished as she pleaded in twisted suffering of body and heart, "I am unloved and wretched! I want to die! I want to die!"

Some unreasoned dam that had stopped inside Edward seemed to burst. He knelt at her side and held her. He could not let her die believing he held her guilty.

"You must go, you upset her," the midwife commanded, trying to shoo him away, but he would not leave her. He caressed Philippa's contorted face, wiping the tears and sweat. The convulsions seemed to ease for a moment.

"You will not die," he told her, as if his command would hold her to the living world.

"You don't love me."

"No—I love you too much," he pleaded gently with her. "It is the burning in my heart that twists my brain and makes me blind. But now I open my eyes—"

"You will not believe me! You want proof of my love! If I die for you now, may the babe prove my faith."

"I am a fool. I need no proof. I feel your love for me in my very soul." Indeed, he could feel a pain in his own belly, which suggested what she felt. "You even give me your pain. Let me take it from you. You will not die. I command it."

He kissed her and held her as she wept with rediscovered happiness. Suddenly, her eyes opened wide, and she gasped. Her breath caught in her throat as her body was wracked with a spasm. Edward clutched her, fearing for her and for God's punishment on him as she labored in torment. Then, like an answer to a question which dare not be asked, a baby's cry filled the chamber.

An infant, wet and slippery, lay upon the woolen cloth of the bed. It was a boy, and cried with instant healthy lungs as the midwife cut the cord amid the joyful cries of the women.

The midwife laid the birth wet bawling infant in Philippa's arm. With her little strength, Philippa managed a weak smile. She looked on the child.

"See? Does he not have my lord's beautiful Plantagenet blue eyes?"

"And indeed his mother's lusty voice," he smiled.

"Shall we name him Edward in honor of his father?" Philippa asked, meeting her husband's gaze.

"No—in honor of his father's father."

"My lord must leave if we have hope to save my lady from bleeding," the mistress midwife chided insistently, "Go!!"

Edward found Richard again in the hall, filled with joy and fear at the same time.

"I have a son!" he beamed with pride.

Richard shared his joy but kept him to the urgent concern. "Edward, you cannot wait if you have hope of saving your uncle. I'll make a caravan ready." Richard started to go to attend to a traveling party, but Edward halted him.

"No, we will go on horse alone. We cannot wait for royal baggage. I'll disguise myself so we may make undisturbed haste. But I will not leave my wife, until I know she's safe."

He began to pace again, restlessly, to wait for fate's judgment.

So, he waited until the first light of morning turned the night outside to the grey of another stormy day. Richard had made horses ready, but waited with him for news of Philippa, until Lea hurried to tell them.

"Your Grace, the bleeding stops. Thy lady lives." Lea pronounced it with exhausted relief in her voice, and added, "If not for her stubborn will, I hate to think."

"Amen to you," answered Edward, relief in his own heart. "Thanks to the good midwives and yourself." He braced Richard, "I'll see to her, then we ride. And pray we are not too late."

4

His trial hastily held and judgment given, Edmund Kent was marched through Winchester town, manacled and only clothed in nightshirt, paraded through the streets to a scaffold in the square before the great cathedral. His accusers and judges, Mortimer and Isabella, and their council allies had all departed the city, so that they might not be associated with the trumped charge and false execution.

Edmund paused at the bottom of the stairs to look up to the drizzling grey sky. He opened his mouth to take a last drink of earthly refreshment, then was shoved, with no ceremony of his rank, up the steps to the block.

While Edmund stood on the scaffold with a headsman waiting, Sir Hugh Terplington read the charge, "Edmund, Earl of Kent, you have been found guilty of Treason. Your execution is hereby ordained and signed by her Highness, Isabella, in the name of her son, Edward." He turned to the headsman. "Executioner, fulfill your charge."

Edmund spoke. "I am found guilty of that which I have not done, yet wherefore is the signature of the King?" He turned to the headsman, "You know me as your Lord, is this head that of traitor?"

The headsman hesitated.

"Fulfill your charge," commanded Terplington.

"I'll not," replied the headsman, unwilling to have this ill-purchased blood splash upon him. He set down his ax and walked down the steps of the scaffold, refusing his duty.

Terplington turned to his Second in frustration. "Go and find an executioner!"

"Where, my lord?" asked the Second.

"Wherever you may," Terplington replied, "I cannot be seen to do it myself!"

Terplington stood upon the rainy platform as his Second searched for a qualified punisher. The crowds who had gathered had begun to jeer. Some had come to see a mighty lord come to lowly, bloody end, but more had felt the injustice of his judges and the grasping host who served them.

The Second returned to the scaffold and shouted to the knight, who had been left with the dirty task.

"I can find no-one with experience who is willing, Sir Terplington!"

Terplington shouted down to him. "Then, find anyone willing! Search the taverns for some old soldier."

The Second ran off again, spattering his boots in the puddles. Many of the gathered crowd began to drift. The rain was cold, and it appeared more and more there would be no bloody entertainment. The onlookers who remained booed and hissed at Terplington.

"Frenchwoman's lackey!" came a shout.

"Mortimer's toad!" came another.

The Second returned with a ragged aging soldier, weaving from drink, and pushed him up the scaffold step, almost having to hold him up.

"I found this yeoman who says he'll do anything for a week's worth of drink," said the Second.

Impatient, Terplington gestured for him to come up. The Second shoved the reluctant drunk up the steps. The crowd jeered and cursed.

Edmund looked into the bleary face of the soldier. "A poor old drunk to do the dirty work of a power drunken queen. Aim well in your cups, old man. I would not you diminished your wages with too many strokes."

The old yeoman bowed as if being honored and blearily picked up the heavy ax.

Edward and Richard had ridden hard from the stony grounds of Cotswold across the plains of ancient druidic monuments to the southern country and had not slept. The rain had stopped as they galloped their horses with snorting breath through the city gates of Winchester and into the cobbled street.

"The King! The King!" Richard shouted as disbelieving witnesses stood aside for them to pass.

Yet, as they reined up their horses in the cathedral square, it was near devoid of human presence. They had arrived too late.

Edmund's head was resting on a pole rising in the middle of the square while the old soldier slumped, lonely drunk on the steps of the scaffold, asleep and alone. Edward sank in his saddle, soaking wet and drenched with loss.

5

As the tolling of the bells still sounded from the Westminster tower, Geoffrey Chaucer looked into the faces of all who had been held in thrall by his story. It was growing late, but none had left or faded away for other tasks of life's call, for they all wondered, old and young, fat and thin, noble or low, how they had come to this day. He seemed weary, and they wondered for a moment, could this be the end of his tale? He looked about at the bustling town, which had grown by halves and then halves again during the reign of his master. How the world had changed under his hand. Finally, he focused again on his audience, ready to reveal the darkest part of his story.

"And so," he told them, allowing them to draw in close again, "the boy had become a man, though hardly yet truly king. It would be at Nottingham's gathering of Parliament that his fate, and indeed, the fate of all of us, would be decided. Mortimer's design was nearly complete, save for one last obstacle. He could not fully rule a kingdom while another sat upon the throne, and so he had made a plan for a remedy."

~~~

CHAPTER NINE

1

17th Day of November, 1330

The baron lords of the realm had made the journey to Nottingham in the midland of the country so that they all might have equal distance for travel and that they might enjoy the hunting in the thick and lush forests at the invitation of the king, after their heavy arguments had finished. Their tents, marked with the flapping flags of their colors, were spread across the plain below the rocky promontory where the fortress castle stood above. All were prepared for intense argument, for this parlay held more in consequence than any before in the four years since they had placed a crown on the young king's brow. Soon was the marking of the eighteenth year since his birth. And among and between them it seemed wherever the gathered lords might go, men-at-arms in the coat colors of Mortimer's house would be on watch, and so too, close at the side of the king, that he might not be free in his movements.

Edward's brother, John, did not travel with the party to Nottingham, but instead had been sent to the Tower in London, it was said, for his safe-keeping from the dust of the roads and pollens of the fir trees. The choice of his lodging was Mortimer's, but reasoned that Windsor was too large to keep him from mischief. He would rule the tower in small confines, in practice, should some ill befall his brother, but unable to leave, even should evil news come.

A retinue of men rode across the drawbridge into the gatehouse of the castle. It was the third day of Parliament and nothing had been settled in the shouts of opposite sides from the beginning of day to its end. Edward rode at the head of the knights with Mortimer beside him, and surrounded by the guard of Mortimer's coat.

Edward was furious, but said nothing as he dismounted within the bailey gate. He dare not speak his real mind in ear-reach of Mortimer, nor any loyal to him. Richard met him as he left his horse to the grooms and they strode away to separate from any that might hear.

"What is the answer?" Richard asked. "Did they listen?"

Edward shook his head and angrily pulled the gloves from his hands, feeling the cold sting of the air which held the promise of snow at nightfall, still half a day hence. "Parliament is a rabble," he barked, "Mortimer has them so divided they quarrel over the slightest matter. We did not even speak."

The Lord Castellan of Nottingham had given over residence of the castle to the king and his retinue for the length of days of Parliament. He only held the stronghold in tenancy by grace of the king for defense of the great royal forests and had moved his own household to temporary residence, so it was only the royal party within the strong keep walls. Mortimer and the Queen Mother, Isabella, held rooms for themselves and their retainers. Edward, the King and his lady consort, Philippa, had been urged to leave their usual compliment of servants, maids, squires and flotsam behind at Windsor for traveling, so that they were as intimate as they had been at Woodstock.

In the solar chamber, Edward and Philippa sat at a table with bread, cheese and porridge spread out, a meager setting, but pleasing that they might be away from all the weighty trappings of their position. Philippa cradled their baby in her arms, allowing him to suckle at her breast, enjoying the stinging pull of his healthy thirst. The infant Prince Edward had grown in fine form, with no flaw nor deform, since his hard birth five months ago.

Lea bustled in upon them and took the child from Philippa. "Mistress!" she scolded, "If you insist on feeding from your own milk, against wiser practice, that is your majestic right, but you mustn't keep it with you so much of the day. Will make the child too attached to mother's ways."

Philippa had refused to give the infant heir over to other nurse maids and had kept him to her own milk, which easily flowed from her. It was not that she disdained the duties of maids, nor their milk, but that in the atmosphere of her husband's house, she felt a general ill-ease at being far separated from her child. She only smiled wanly as Lea carried the baby away "coo-cooing" to it, doting as a mother might. Lea had never been with a man, nor family, and had been as a nun all these years in Philippa's service since she was an infant.

"I am chastised," Philippa whispered to Edward, so that her servant could not hear. "I think she wishes it were her own."

Edward smiled but was not closely listening, lost in his own thought. Philippa reached to touch his hand, worried for him.

"You're in a far land, husband. You do not eat."

"I wonder if I was held too close by my mother," he pondered aloud.

"It has made you no less a prince in my eye—and now you have a wife for closer holding." She leaned on his chair and wrapped her arms around him, kissing his neck. "But there is more that troubles you. Won't you burden me with some of your heavy baggage?"

Edward held up a folded parchment with dark stains.

"What is that?" Philippa asked. It did not appear like any official document but hand-scribed in shaky writ.

"It is a poem my father etched in his prison tower. It never reached my hand as I allowed myself to be turned by false love."

"Read it."

"It is Latin. I studied it to learn the law and history, but now my father reaches out to me." He held it to the light to read. "Oh, who that heard how once they praised my name, could think from those tongues slanders came. I see Thy rod, and, Lord, I am content. Sweet Jesus, humble here I bend and confess my sins, so that from my son do pardon send, and forgive, that when I die, grieve, that my love shall live."

Edward fell silent as Mortimer entered with his mother.

"A cozy couple," Mortimer remarked on them together.

"He grows more insufferable every day," Philippa whispered to Edward. She had not relayed to him the odious way the high-rising baron had been with her now that they were together in close quarters.

Mortimer bowed gallantly to Philippa, taking her reluctant hand to kiss, but she pulled it away, ungraciously.

"Do you not bow to the king before his wife?" she asked sharply.

"Your husband knows his position. He needs no reminder from me." Mortimer's contempt was now bald and clearly intended, with only the barest patina of diplomacy.

"Can naught be done to curb this arrogance?" Philippa whispered again to Edward, in the directness of her young care for her husband's honor, but risking driving him to the passionate impatience of his nature which might overrun his caution.

Edward, too, felt the sting of Mortimer's now easy disregard of his station and the betrayal of his love and all the lives turned to wormy grave by false witness and deception. In a flash of temper, he gripped a dull cheese knife and rose to face Mortimer, but Mortimer's hand rested ready on the hilt of the sword that he now wore, always at his side.

This might have been the moment of the story's end, but Edward regained himself and cut a slice of the cheese set out for their refreshment.

Philippa rose and curtsied to the marcher lord with all the decorum she could muster and left them.

Mortimer smiled at his effect. He reached to take the cheese slice from Edward to eat it himself, as he might intend to devoir to himself all that belonged to the young king before him.

"A man cannot help but admire her spirit." Mortimer grinned. "Though how quickly do ladies' favors change."

He kissed Isabella in front of her son, that he might know he possessed her.

"You need to smile more, young prince," he said, before striding away quickly, that Edward might not reach to strike at him, and was gone.

Edward was now alone with his mother. Words would not come as he jabbed the useless cheese knife into the table, wishing it was a sword.

Isabella rested her hand on his cheek. "It makes me sad to have lost the happy child you once were."

Edward pulled away from her hand, which now felt course and hot, where in youth's innocence it had meant love, now, only betrayal. "I would grin ear to ear at the sight of Mortimer's head and drawn quarters displayed on the four gates of London.

"How do you speak so?!" she bristled. "Mortimer is best friend in our cause against the greedy barons."

"Are you so blinded by your need, Mother, that you cannot see how he twists your noble aim with flattering lies?"

"Am I such a withered old hag in my son's eyes? Has Isabel's beauty fallen into such disrepair he can so easily discard her?"

He could not hold back the doubt and self-examination which had been gnawing at his brain like a rat at the cheese, even while he stood before the lords in conclave, arguing for the rightful position which had been usurped from him by his own acquiescence.

"Mother, your beauty is a curse! Vanity is my family's curse. It brought down my father and I cannot deny that it runs hot in my own veins. Would I could drain it out!"

"Now my son curses me?" Isabella railed, lost in her own concern. "He abandons me like his father before!"

"Any mirror will tell that you are as fair as ever! It is the strong spirit within which has withered and dried," he said with a pain of the loss of his once pure admiration for what she had represented to him.

Yet, Isabella only turned cold, unhearing. "Then it is only the reflection in Mortimer's eye Isabel may trust."

He took her hand in his to plead, remembering when it consoled his worry and soothed his pain as a child.

"Mother, you might have been great! Men followed you, not because you were beautiful, but because they believed in you, as I believed. It was you who filled me with dreams of kingdoms united where men might live by the codes of their more noble natures. But, I beg you, turn away from this man I once honored as a great knight, who has turned the ideal into a jest! Whose unbound lust for power will plunge this land into war upon itself!"

"Gentle Mortimer is indeed Isabel's last friend when even a son turns on his mother," she answered him with a distance from him and from the world which he could not fathom.

He could only look upon her with a pain of regret for what once was, knowing now they were at the cross. "Then, we are lost."

Isabella left her son's censure to make her way to her own private apartment. Philippa hurried to catch her.

"Maman, Isabel—" Philippa said, hoping to mend any issue between them.

"Queen Isabel," was the sharp correcting response with the weight of demand.

"I beg your pardon, Your Majestic Grace, I would not for the world hope to offend you."

"Then, do not." Isabella was curt and cold as stone.

"Have I caused you some injury, or insult?" Philippa asked in innocent hope of a bridge between them.

"Does the fresh-blushing rose insult the wilting bloom?"

Philippa was mystified.

"I had hoped our child would cheer you and bring us together, but I fear I have caused you some ill."

Isabella now gently stroked Philippa's tender cheek.

214

"Tres belle. Beware beauty, my child. It will purchase for you great advantage in life, but the cost to be paid is collected with increased tithing."

Philippa thought she understood, but was sad that one she so admired for her strength would dwell on the subject and let it fill her days. On her journey across the sea, betrothed to a new royal husband, it was Isabella that she had thought she might model herself as queen, but now she wondered. She wanted to understand her cousin mother.

"You love Mortimer, but he is not your husband."

Isabella was challenged by the directness of the question by one who she would not allow to judge her, but instead of the angry rebuke she might have given on other occasion, she answered.

"He loves me. My husband did not." Isabella was sharp as a needle and wounded all at once. "You have been given a rare gift. My son loves you. I am forgotten."

Philippa attempted to assure her as much as she might. "Love is not diminished by division, but increased by the addition. Is that not true? I look at my son and see Edward all the more."

"I envy you, then. I look at my son, and see his unnatural father the more." Isabella was as honest of her feelings with Philippa as she might ever be, and then even more honest. "Beware of Mortimer, do not encourage him. He is not the one I will blame."

Philippa left the troubling congress with her mother-by-law, the clear warning echoing in her soul. She hurried along a corridor toward her chamber, still guarded by one of Mortimer's men, where she might escape the intrigue of her kinship, yet before she could reach it, Mortimer caught her and grasped her arm, with no regard for his place and hers.

"Release me, before I have your hand removed from its arm," she commanded with a haughtiness intended to hide her fear.

"My lady exalts in her majesty."

"I am Queen, am I not?"

Mortimer was only amused by the claim. He had lived by his own rules and relished that he might now put them into action upon the world that had denied him.

"Titles can be given or they may be taken," he said with a darkness of soul that would claim them all. "True right of power and indeed all things worth having must be won." He shoved her against the wall and kissed her on the lips, pressing upon her, that she might feel his strength. As she struggled against him, the guard at her door nearby stood unmoving, taking no action to protect her honor so flagrantly tossed away.

Philippa felt her powerlessness against him, all the while mindful that it was not he who would be judged. She did what she could to fend him, but her struggle was perhaps the grasping lord's intent.

"Call to your husband and see if the boy has courage enough to defend his honor," he growled with a smile of puerile satisfaction. Philippa pushed him off, though by her own effort or at his will may be debated.

"I will defend mine own, to death if must be," she looked into his black eye, where she could see her own face reflected. "My lord, you already possess another man's wife. What do you want of me she does not provide?"

"Why, that quality more precious than gold which men of my years seek with intense fervor, but lose as soon as it is found."

"Are you so crooked, my lord, you can only speak in riddles?"

"Innocence, dear lady," he finally answered with a revelation of his darkest soul. "Only in the purity of youth's beauty is the soot of age washed clean."

Philippa felt his powerful warrior's arms upon her and knew she could offer no defense if he acted upon unsheathed lust to take everything that belonged to her. She drew upon all the strength of courage she could find to face him with a last dignity.

"And the drainage water that did the washing is turned as black as that it washed. I understand you very well, my lord, and I am flattered you are so honest with me. Yet, I still prefer to wash my own husband's back."

She pushed against him with all her will and made a dash for her chamber door. The guard did not stop her and she managed to open it. She slipped inside and slammed it, hoping it might offer protection.

Mortimer only laughed. If he had wanted to stop her, he could have ordered his guard, who would have obeyed him, or could have held her, but his passion was not for the pleasures of flesh nor need for his own sensation, but for the effect of his will. And he was pleased.

Edward stormed up the tower steps, turning and turning to the western battlement walk, throwing open the protecting door so that it hit with a thud against the wall. He paced beside the arrow loops which faced out across the plain where the tents were gathered. The sky was cloudless and the air crisp and cold as the sun set beyond the forest trees, casting crimson shards across the world's edge. He roared at the sky with fists clenched in a growl of pent up rage.

Richard watched him pacing from the door of the stair. He knew this mood. He had come to learn to measure his friend, that he might give better counsel.

"The lion roars," he mocked with an intended shade of mirth. "Small use growling at the sky. You'll only make it rain."

"If it would cleanse me of this pestilence I have allowed to fester, it should pour for forty days and nights!" He continued his pacing as if each step of his foot might step upon an unseen answer to his plight. "My silence has made me a prisoner in my own house." As he paced, he found a stick of wood used to prop the door open. He picked it up and twirled it like a quarterstaff. His thought returned to earlier, simpler days, when he was just a boy who met a traitor.

"I am Mortimer's lunch. He feasts on my carcass like a buzzard before the animal is dead." He considered the stick. "God, Richard, do you remember that day in the tower yard you knocked me down? When we first met?"

Richard was puzzled why he might think of such a time so far from their present world. "Yes. But I hardly see how it will help our current circumstance."

Edward located another wood shard and tossed it to his friend.

"I would give my crown and all the weight of state for one more innocent child's game of stick and hoop. Knock me down," he commanded.

Richard was confounded by his digression. "His Grace cannot be serious."

Edward gestured for Richard to come at him, accepting no argument.

"Come on. Have at me! As if we were at lists! Knock me from the wall!"

Richard could find no escape but to humor his whim and came at him with the stick. It was as if they were practicing in the training box, but Edward seemed determined, as if all depended on the outcome of a mock battle. Edward dodged. Richard spun and feinted. They teetered on the stony escarpment as the clacking of the sticks echoed off the walls. As Edward moved to his feint, Richard shouldered him like a bull, knocking him to the stone.

Edward sat upon the stone, spent and thoughtful. Then, he giggled, like a mirth from the release of a deep knot. Richard could not fathom what was in his mind. Surely, he had allowed himself to be knocked down, so a test of his skills was not the object of the exercise.

"I've heard madness runs in royal blood," said Richard, puzzling.

Still laughing, Edward extended his hand for Richard to pull him up from the stones. But as he rose, his hand gripped his friend's with a sinew-taught grip and burning fire in his eyes.

"Tomorrow at Parliament, I shall give Mortimer's ambition such a blow, will knock him into history's dust! And my son will have a king for a father!"

He swung the wooden stick against the stone parapet so that it snapped with a crack, and flung the pieces from his hand over the wall. It tumbled to mossy walls of foundation below, where the lichens and snails clung to the damp crevices.

2

18th Day of November, 1330

The lords of England were gathered within the freshly constructed church meant to serve the growing village of Nottingham. It was made with the new fashion of building with pointed arches and windows of colored glass which might cast light into the darker reaches of men's souls. Yet, on this day, the third of the gathering of parliament, it was not God who was celebrated, but government by men who might have a say in the whims of those set above them, by His wish and fortune.

Edward stood at the pulpit below the banner of parliamentary herald, signifying this was not a place of royal right, but the common will. Angered voices filled the nave, rising to the high vaults, as if the sculpted saints in masonic carved relief on the columns were speaking rather than the assembled. Mortimer and Isabella sat to one side of the aisle at the head of many who had followed them and received benefit from them. On the other side were barons and commons, many of whom who had once followed in belief of better promises, but were friends no more.

"My lords and gentlemen," Edward spoke out, trying to calm their attention from the heated discussion. On the front row of the benches opposite Isabella were Lancaster, Montagu, and the Earls of Suffolk and Warwick. An empty place was kept with the banner mark of Edmund of Kent, the three lions of Henry Plantagenet, that his presence would be felt in his death.

The bickering of voices calmed to hear the speech of the young king, his first public address before them marked by this day. Mortimer especially pricked his attention to the boy's intent in his address, for it had been kept from his advance inquiry

"You grumble here about the lands and powers given to the new Earl of March," Edward nodded to Mortimer. Half the gathered host cheered and stomped their feet, half sat upon their hands. The creation of the new title had been a chief point of division, as it set Mortimer not as equal to his follow guardians of the marcher boarders of Wales, but above them, and Edward had been forced to sign it by his mother and the regal council at which she and Mortimer held majority.

"And you have honest reason to complain," he continued, allowing the opposite side to jeer and call, "but I am forced by this council you have placed over me! Such is your right under the Great Charter to which I freely subscribe." Cheers now roared from all.

"Yet, if you are now unhappy, I offer a solution."

Mortimer sat coolly as he spoke, with his plan already in place. He knew this day would come and he had not been idle in his prospect of it, but he was surprised at Edward's assured manner before the distemperate, unruly lords. He had hoped the young king would grow to be as feckless and occupied with the trappings and pleasures of his state as his father had been, granted by accident of blood the great chair upon which he rested, but this boy was of another mind. Mortimer's fate and his choice ahead were reflected in his dark eye as he listened.

"As I have attained my eighteenth birthday, and have a child as sign of having left youth behind," Edward continued, "I ask that you disband the Council of Regency. Untie my hands! Give to me the whole crown, that I may forge a just balance between king and the people. Together, may we right what has been wrong! I await your answer."

3

Edward hesitated in his history, having arrived at the present place. He looked to the monk who had listened to his story in considered attention, with only the occasional inquiry to clarify his understanding.

"Is there more, my lord?" the monk asked.

Edward looked to the face of care-lined fleshy folds beyond the flickering taper wick, a kindness in the eyes. The last candle had burned down to a melted stub, which yet still shed a shifting glow into the stone-arched reaches of the chapel. The cobalt gloaming of advancing morn shown outside the single rose filigreed window in the wall.

The distant crying of his infant son intruded on Edward's reverie, drifting into the stones of the chapel. He was reminded of the time.

"That, I suppose, is the present question, good Father. Is there more, or is this the last dawn to see?" He glanced to the window light. "You have heard how I came to this moment, my good friar. Have you any advise for me?"

The monk thought a moment on all he had heard and how he might be of best service in weighty matters far above his station.

"How may a simple brother who has spent near all his existence upon God's fertile soil in the cloisters advise a king?" He answered with care, wishing he could do more. "I am only authorized to offer His forgiveness for sins confessed."

Edward smiled in wary resolve and pulled his robe close around his shoulders. "Let forgiveness be enough, then. All else will come soon enough." He tugged one of the rings from his finger, a deep green stone of cut sparkling facets clutched by gold lions. He held it for the monk. "For your good service."

The monk stared at the offering. His eyes seemed to mist with appreciation. "I cannot accept it, Sire. I have sworn to forfeit worldly goods and cares."

Edward turned the ring in his hand. "It was my father's. And his before. It was gifted to Henry, the first of my family to sit upon a throne. As I may be the last this night, I might hope for it to bring a shift of fortune in the gift, if God would not consider it bribery."

"Perhaps a small coin, with your likeness on it, my lord," the monk suggested with humble graciousness.

"I have none with me," answered the young king, smiling at the impoverished priest's modesty. "I would be glad to be lightened of the weight of it. The lighter to arrive at the narrow gates, now that I have been forgiven my sins. I insist you take it. Divide the value among your Order in service of your mission. If I am to fall, better it were in your hands than those that would take it."

The monk accepted the gift. "I will find a purpose for it and pray for your hopeful prospect, my lord."

Edward met with Richard in the corridor leading from the chapel. Richard had been through all the castle to find they were without protection. He was breathless from climbing stairs.

"Edward, all the armaments have been closed up in guarded stores," he reported. "The Nottingham lord sleeps in town on some pretext, and his familiars have been sent away. The castle is all Mortimer's."

Edward knew Mortimer's mind better than he knew his own. Parliament would give an answer by sunrise. If the answer was "aye", Mortimer's day would be passed, and it was tonight he must make his move.

"Then, if we don't wish to die in our beds tonight," Edward said, his mind in dark thought, "we must get word to what friends we have outside."

"But Nottingham is the best fortified keep in England. Even if they were to lay siege, it would take days."

"Then it may be, good Richard, that we make our last stand for honor with scullery knives."

Edward once again entered Philippa's chamber without announcement, that they might be private.

The queen consort was unfamiliar with her husband's dreadful concern.

"Has my husband returned again to take his pleasure?" she joked, hoping that his unescorted visit meant they might share each other. He longed for intimacy with her, observing her soft form in her night dressing, and willing smile, but he was gripped by a more urgent cause.

"This will not be a night to please any of us," he said, sadly, then commanded her in a stern voice, "Close yourself in your servant's chamber and bolt the door with a strong weight. Open it to no voice but mine."

She now read the darkness of his temper. "Edward, will you not tell me what is wrong?"

"If you love me as I love you, do as I say." He touched her sweet face with a caressing hand, but firm intent. "No voice but mine."

She could now read the fear in his eyes as he gazed upon her, perhaps holding a wish that it would not be the last. She was not a fool, nor foolish, and realized what may be upon them.

"Your voice is the only music my ears will hear."

She kissed him, hard, as if to make it last until the crow of doom's call, and he strode from the room, slamming the door behind. Philippa hurried to the door and threw the bolt. She disturbed Lea in her antichamber with hasty knocking.

"What is my lady's urgency?" her servant asked, awakened from a drifted sleep.

"Gather all we might require for the night, so that we need call for no supply," Philippa commanded her. Then Philippa lifted her babe from its swaddling cradle.

"Why do you disturb him, Lady?"

"Hush!" Philippa insisted, not wishing to explain all. "And make haste. We keep close company tonight."

Lea watched in dismay as her mistress tossed discarded clothing onto her bed and pulled the covering over them, that they might make a lump. She could not fathom such behavior until she read the fear in her lady's face, and at last understood. Philippa ushered Lea with her into her own servant's wardrobe and slammed that door closed, so that they were alone.

4

Montagu stood upon the field outside of his tent, looking up at the silhouetted fortress on the cliff above. The walls nearest the inner keep clung to the hillock of sandy stone, crabbed with thickets of scrub and Black Alder. He was thinking of the effort an assault would take to breach the castle. It stood on a narrow ridge which rose along the flow of the River Trent. At its highest point, it was two-hundred feet above the firm midlands earth, and on the southern end of this ridge, was situated the motte and keep of the upper bailey, enclosed by a mighty curtain wall. To the north was the middle bailey, also enclosed by a lower stone wall and all surrounded to the south by an outer enclosure of earth and timber palisade. There was only one gate to the north, approached by a long winding road rising by degrees up the promontory. To the west was the park of plain and patch forest, while to the north and east, the defended ville of Nottingham borough. The castle had never been taken by force in its days since the Romans departed. Sieged by King Richard of the Lionheart for three days, it only fell because those inside changed allegiance and surrendered. He despaired of reaching the king by force.

He was drawn from this reverie as Lancaster rode down from the gates and looked much aged as he held up at Montagu's tent. He dismounted with difficulty, leaving the thick stuffed pillow tied to his saddle.

"God! I creak!" Lancaster cursed.

Montagu tried to assist him, but the proud man shrugged him off.

"I'll die standing on my own feet, or I'll not die at all. But I will see this Mortimer go before, I swear it."

"Were you able to speak to the King? Does he revel at our decision?" Montagu asked with uncertain hope, for no answer had come from their herald sent before with the message that the king had been proclaimed in his own right, by acclamation. In fact, a dark silence had fallen since the shouting and cheers of the vote had faded.

"They would not open the gate, nor give message."

Montagu returned his gaze upon the castle, his most dread worry confirmed. "So, Mortimer prepares his move. I have several men ready for the king's aid, but 'tis a mighty rock against a small number."

The lords were forbidden by concord to bring armed regiments to gatherings of parliament, beyond a number needed to secure their personal fate, lest the greater barons of them might force their wills upon the lesser. Such were the foundations of the parlay set in the charter signed by John, to meet the object of decision without bloodshed. Yet, Mortimer had set his loyal guards to a force amounting to a small army in the guise of securing the safety of all, and had ringed the encampment. Many of Mortimer's men had been conscripted among the Welsh lands he held in sway, and could not be communicated with in courtly tongue. It had already caused more than a few violent exchanges in drunken bloody brawls.

"Warwick has three-hundred strong at Coventry, but I fear if they march, Mortimer would unleash his number here about us." Lancaster assessed, equaling Montagu's concern.

"Then, we sleep with our swords." The younger lord offered his tent for discussion where inside were gathered a few others of their confidence, and they withdrew from the enclosing cold and observance.

5

Edward had urged Richard to discover the full prospect of their circumstance, and Richard had found Edward in a darkened hall of the lower tower, near the larder stores where they had agreed to meet.

"I have inquired of all the house help and cannot find a way of getting a message outside the walls," Richard reported, breathless from roaming the fortress. "We're boxed, Edward. Only ghosts roam the walks."

They were startled by the clack of a door latch and the opening creak of the portal to the cellars, and froze as if they might have been discovered. Yet, instead of armed men of ill intent, it was the monk confessor who emerged from the lower floors. He bowed when he realized he had disturbed the king.

"Beg pardon, Sire. I hope I have not alarmed you."

Edward, breathing lighter, greeted him, as he might an old friend, though had only known him for an hour. "Still at your devotions, good brother?"

"Your confession has weighed heavily on my mind, Sire. I have been in constant commune with the heavenly Father since we parted." The monk's fingers, made crooked by the ague of the joints which froze and twisted them in nodules of age, played with the ring Edward had gifted him, still in his hand. "Perhaps, I have some means to return kindness."

"How so?" Edward was curious now at the monk's intended mystery.

"An answer to your prayer, my gracious lord." He gestured to the open doorway to the lower passages as if inviting, with a gentle whisper that they might not be heard by any who might spy. "Come, and have wine with me?"

Richard was impatient with the priest, for he did not know of what had passed with the king.

"We have no time for frivolity, Monk."

Yet, the brother of the Cistercian Order would not be deterred. If they had known him for any time and had inquired, they would have discovered that though he had been at monastic devotion in quiet solitude for long years, was no stranger to adventure.

He signaled secretively for them to follow him. Edward and Richard exchanged a glance of curiosity. Edward was sanguine and intrigued.

"Perhaps all that's left for us is a good drunk."

With a taper light held in jittering hand, the confessor led the way down the stair spirals into the bowels of the castle where the walls melded and joined in the foundation with the sandy stone of the mountain upon which it stood.

"You have a nature I have rarely encountered in one of your calling, brother monk. What brought you to your devotion?" Edward asked as they continued down into the dark undercroft.

"I was born in a good family, Your Grace, but misspent my youth. I had a desire for danger and sought it out."

"Then, you have seen service in arms, Monk?" Richard asked, his interest now piqued.

"I have wielded a sword, good master, and have slew men, but I saw in the Holy Sepulchre a light which led me on another path. I joined the Cistercian brothers, serving the Templars, before their disgrace."

"More surprises, with every step," Edward laughed. "Would you had your comrades at arms lodged below. Have you been to Jerusalem?"

"Aye, my lord. I have made the pilgrimage—for my own sins."

The stair at last opened on a low-ceilinged space that reached beyond the flame of the confessor's candle, into dark corners where the foundations embedded in the cliff rock it perched on.

"I have forsworn all violence, Sire, lest I be judged by the same flame which consumed the knights of the cross pattée, all flesh and cursing. Yet, it has been my good fortune while here at Nottingham to be given mastery of the wines. For, though I am avowed to drink naught but the sacrament blood of Our Savior, I do take much pleasure in the odor of the fermenting fruit."

The flickering light of the candle glowed upon several open wine barrels, with the scum of musk and fruit skin floating on the top. Rats scuttled away as the confessor set his candle near a half-empty barrel resting on a mass of rock protruding from the floor. He grabbed hold of the barrel with his craggy hands.

"Would it not be better to drink from a cup, Friar?" Richard quipped, thinking their time before death might be better spent.

"If my lords would give hand," the monk insisted, as they realized he intended to move the object.

Puzzled by his never-ending intrigue without a clearer explanation, Edward and Richard also grasped the barrel to lift it, and roll it aside. Tilted out of the way, the monk was able to remove the old boards that the barrel had rested on, laid over the rock beneath. As he took them away, a dark hole was revealed. It was but two feet wide, and disappeared into the mountain.

Edward and Richard stared in amazement. It was a passage, a cave of natural formation, but carved with steps for a distance they could observe, until vanishing in blackness from the candle's glimmer.

"In Saxon days," the monk explained, "when the fortress was constructed, a means of secret escape was much used. In these more peaceful times, it has been forgotten. The castle has gained such a reputation that a sally port was of small need."

The confessor held the candle closer so that they might see farther down into the hole. The stair steps descended into a winding, narrow tunnel.

"Where does it go"? Richard asked.

"It leads to a cave that exits to an underground spring at the base of the mount."

"Friar, your prayers are generous indeed!" Edward grinned in surprise and delight at the discovery. Then his mind thought back to a night on the moors of the northern borders where he had nearly come to a greeting with death, but for an earlier confessor who had sacrificed himself for his young king.

"Once before, one of your brethren intervened to save me. Perhaps the Divine has chosen me for a purpose, after all." Edward looked on the kindly face and smiled. "You must be very close to God, Father. I'll make you a bishop!"

"A Priorship would be more to my liking, Sire," he demurred. "There are too many worldly matters in Bishopric."

"If we survive, you can make me Bishop." Richard offered in jest, at last seeing hope.

The confessor grabbed up a cold torch from the floor and lit it from his candle, the flame embracing and warming the oil tar. Edward took the torch from him and handed it to Richard.

"Hold me to it," he met his friend's eyes, now shared in hopeful promise. "Make your way best you can and get to Montagu".

Richard understood and gamely began to climb down into the rough, narrow hole.

Once he had found footing, he looked back up at them with a grin. "If I don't return with assistance in time, you may banish me forever on forfeit of my head."

"If you are not timely," Edward replied with all the weight of their situation, "you may have mine to keep you company.

With that, Richard disappeared into the abyss. Edward watched him go, as the light from his torch was visible for a while, then it, too, was gone from sight in the twisting hole.

6

Richard picked his way through the rocky cave, moving as quickly as the cramped black passage would allow. His torch withered, bereft of air in the narrow confine, so that he could scarce see his own feet below. The steps which had begun when he entered had ended and his footing was on knobby stone of uneven level, steep and turning. His hands upon the walls felt the cool surface of bare stone with loosening grains of substance, the occasional slime of some wet rivulet and the movement of unknown creatures who sustained themselves in the underworld. Where he was going he did not know, whether to air and field or directly into the hell of burning fire.

Around a high table in the room next to Isabella's bedchamber in the upper reaches of the keep, Mortimer was gathered with his intimate retainers, Sir Terplington and Monmouth, Mortimer's two sons, William and Henry, and two Captains-at-Arms.

Isabella herself was at the opposite end of the table, already dressed for the night in a robe over her nightgown. She was distracted and seemed disinterested in their discussions. Spread upon the table between them all was a map of the shires and boroughs of the midlands of England. The distances between them were the focus of their considerations.

"All garrisons are prepared to move on our signal, my lord Earl." Terplington pointed to a spot on the map with a color marker of the king's loyal banners. "Warwick has three-hundred pike and archers at Coventry, but he hesitates. Suffolk has called on his vassal counties to yield a thousand, but they move slowly to post."

Mortimer considered the map with satisfaction. He had moved his pieces in place well in advance of this day, knowing it would be his last and best chance. A long game of move and counter he had played since waiting for his turn for the headsman's ax at the Tower. Lancaster had been neutered and Kent removed. The young boy who claimed the throne was left alone to beg for his right, before the cowering barons, and only he saw the full view of the table.

"Time falls to us, then," he said with a simple satisfaction. "When we have finished the business tonight, signal our commander in Nottingham below. Lancaster, Montagu, Warwick and Suffolk must fall before sunrise. We will announce the dissolution of Parliament and my naming as Lord Protector at high sun."

He turned to his sons, already equipped with arms and eager for the prize which was to come to them with his ascension. "Then, you'll quick to lay siege at Coventry and box the lower counties. When all is secure, we march on London, where the breathless brother prince has been installed to play his part, standing at his mother's side."

The conspirators looked around the table with excitement and trepidation, fixing one another with oath and promise. Their plan would shake the world.

Terplington looked to Isabella, then to Mortimer, awaiting the command he knew was needed.

"But first we must remove the royal impediments."

Mortimer looked to Isabella. Her eyes were unrevealing of her intent.

"Isabella?"

She was distant, as if in someone else's dream. She had loved Mortimer, used him, guided him, and now followed him. She must choose.

A shimmer of dim, muted light from some unknown source greeted Richard's searching eyes as he felt a fresh brush of air to replace the foul dampness of the tunnel he had been following. His torched flared with the breeze to reveal the cramped stone shaft opened into a larger cavern. Now, were steps roughly hewn from the sandy rock of the deep cavern, where one misstep might lead to black abyss, but he sensed his downward egress had near reached its goal.

Soon, the cave simply ended. There was a small door of weed-grown boards. He pushed, but it did not move. This must be the object of his journey, but he worried that should it be firm-bolted from the other side, he might be found as a dried corpse in years hence. He pushed again and it appeared to give a little under his force. He leaned with all his weight upon it, bracing against the stone into which it was set. It moved again, and again by degrees, until he was free.

The camp fires of a long night's vigil had burned down to coals as Richard hurried among the tents of the gathered lords, avoiding Mortimer's black-coated sentinels. Finally, he located the tent he sought, calling out in hushed secret.

"Montagu!"

The tent flap was thrown back by the suspicious baron with his sword ready, poised to strike, but he paused with surprise at seeing Richard.

"Bury?!" He tried to fathom his presence. Had he performed some magic trick? "We thought you were closed up with the king."

"So thought we," Richard said with a breathless excitement. "But I have come through an unknown passage."

Montagu whispered urgently into the tent, "Lord Earl, quickly."

Lancaster appeared from within. They had all waited and none had gone abed this night.

Richard told them with as much force as he dare. "We must gather an armed force, and quickly. King and lady are in grave danger. The whole of the castle has been made to Mortimer's order. The king is alone, without guard."

"I have men ready," was Montagu's reply, "but we dare not take a large number lest we breach secrecy. Lancaster, will you with us?" He turned to the aging peer.

"Nay, I am too feeble. You must fly with the speed of youth. I will gather our allies here in the field." He braced them with warm encouragement. "It lies with you, to save us."

Montagu disappeared into his tent for a moment and reappeared, girding his sword and fortifying his belt with daggers. Lancaster gathered his own sword girth and gave it to Richard.

"For the King, as sign of my good friendship," Lancaster urged in hope, "Long may he live."

It was more a wish, than salutation. Richard and Montagu hurried off through the camp to other tents.

Lancaster looked up to the castle on the hill, standing dark sentinel against the sky, with one lighted window glowing, and dreaded its portent.

In the chamber apartments above, Mortimer waited for Isabella's acknowledgement.

"Have I your consent, Isabella? When your son is dead and the infant becomes King, I need your signature on the proclamation to dissolve the government."

Isabella was silent.

"Isabella! Have I your consent?"

Still, she was silent. This turn was no surprise, but now that it had come, she could not fully grasp it in her mind.

Mortimer understood it was a hard choice, to finally meet the inevitable end of a long and singular path. He tried to soften it. "You will have another son beside you. And a grandchild to hold."

Isabella looked up to him as with a distant faint wish.

"Will his killing be kind?" she asked.

"As kind as swiftness will allow," he answered, holding his impatience. "Will you consent?"

She seemed unable or unwilling to decide. Her mind was filled with memories and questions at the same time. Son or lover?

"I am very tired. When will you come to bed?" was all she would say.

"Will you consent? Make your choice."

She drew with her finger absently on the table.

"Isabel?"

"I will sign your paper. But come to bed soon. I am very tired." She turned and padded in bare feet to her bedchamber, drawing the curtain, and shutting it from her mind.

"The lady seems much distracted. Will she hold?" Terplington questioned, observing her. He had followed her and worshiped her, since only a bare youth himself, but this was another queen he did not recognize.

"She grows worse," Mortimer answered, his concern divided between the woman and his purpose. "Her humors flicker like a candle. But she will hold long enough. Once the deed is done, there is no retreat."

"How then, shall it be done? We cannot leave proof of violence on the body?"

Mortimer looked among them, drawing certain. "What was good for the father will serve for the son."

Mortimer nodded his signal to them and with no further need for instruction, Terplington took the two captains. Monmouth took the sons with him.

Mortimer called after them. "See you don't harm the child. And bring the tender young queen to me."

Edward waited impatiently in the croft among the pungent barrels, occasionally shoving his candle into the hole, looking for movement. There was nothing from below but an unholy silence. He anxiously notched at the candle taper with a carving knife the friar used for cutting vine stems. He wondered if it might serve as a weapon, but its blade was brittle and rotted with the iron crust, so that it might break once put to the test upon flesh and bone. He had sent the monk to look after himself, away from danger. He would not wish to have another confessor sacrificed to his conscience. He wondered if Richard had found an exit, or was forever lost to some dark-dwelling monster.

Far from Edward's hearing, Richard led Montagu and six armed men into the tunnel opening, guarded by the weed and vine grown gate. Another was left to keep watch that they might not be discovered and assaulted from behind, but then to follow, when their intent was secure.

With torches, they made their way up the treacherous steps. The fluttering flames outlined the shape of the cavern of uneven walls tapering into a narrow, steep-rising tunnel. Among the men in service to Montagu was the young squire who found the Scots, made a knight on the battlefield, Sir Thomas Rokeby. He had greeted Richard with old familiarity and remembrance to good times on the field, but now the king's advisor was intent on his footing.

"The passage narrows ahead," Richard said, turning to see that the others were close behind, and the last man joining them. "It will be difficult with arms."

"We shall squeeze through a cheese grate if need be," Montagu replied, fixing Richard with an intensity of purpose. "Lead on."

They climbed a few more steps and reached where the narrow hole started up, but to Richard's surprise there were twin caves which forked from the same spot. He stopped to examine them, thrust his torch into each. They were unfamiliar now in the light from fresh torches.

"There are two passages. I don't know which I took! It was dark."

"You cannot tell by the shape?" Montagu asked.

"I was in a hurry. And it was black as doom. I could only feel with my hands."

"Look for sign of your passing," Montagu urged him. They both searched the rocks for some disturbance. Richard placed his hand on the stone of each passage to see if he could tell a difference, but he could not.

"I see nothing."

Montagu stood perplexed that they might take the wrong shaft and be lost. "It be blasted black as the devil's own soul in here, even with burning light."

"Should we divide?" Rokeby asked of Montagu.

Montagu thought of the plan, but came to a clear mind on it. "We are already such small numbers. No—it be all, or nought. Richard of Bury, if we would save our king, you must choose the way."

The door of the king's apartment chamber burst open and Terplington, with the two captains, stormed in. They were intent upon mischief and one of the captains carried a fireplace poker, which glowed upon the end with a red purple heat.

With a growl of discovery, Terplington grasped at the lump under the covers on the bed. A boy's voice shrieked in fright, but it was not the king.

Terplington held up by the scruff of his night shirt the king's page who had decided to take advantage of the empty cushion while his lord was away.

"Where's thy master, Page?!"

"Faith, I know not, sir. He has not been abed. I only thought to warm the sheets for him." He trembled, that he might be punished for it.

"Lucky we don't warm your sheets, little toad." Terplington held the terrified lad close to the searing poker, then with a gruff grunt threw him back upon the bed.

In Philippa's private chamber, the door also was caved by force when no answer to entreaty was answered. The huge Monmouth led Mortimer's sons into the chamber. They spied the lump there, but quickly understood the ruse. They grabbed at the sheets, but came up with nought but wadded cloth.

"There isn't but the lady's laundry," said William Mortimer.

Monmouth looked around the room. His eye fell on the closed door to the servant's cloak chamber. He moved to open it, but found it barred. He butted against it with his large frame, but it stood fast.

Within the small antechamber, Philippa and Lea cowered together on Lea's cot while the door was rattled. They had piled a chest and table against it, fearing it was but a small defense. Philippa held her infant son close to her, keeping him quiet, hoping that silence might be their best savior.

Monmouth's gruff voice came through the boards of the wood, seeping through the unsealed cracks between them like an evil smoke.

"Are you within, Your Grace? Your husband bids you come to him."

Monmouth and the others listened for an answer or any sign of their object.

"Is it possible she's elsewhere in hiding?" William asked, thinking the closed door might only be another deception.

Monmouth listened at the door a moment longer, and rattled it with the hilt of his sword, but still no sign came from behind it.

"Then we search elsewhere. Where could a lady hide?" Monmouth stepped from the door, but as he turned, resolved that their charge to bring the young queen must take them elsewhere, the soft moan of a baby's cry came from the chamber.

Philippa tried to keep her son silent, holding him inside her cloak, but no effort short of suffocating him would stop him. She quickly held him to her breast that he might suckle, and was silent again.

Monmouth held his spot as the others rallied to depart. He listened for more of the sound he thought he had heard. There was no more. The soldier captains, men more attuned to battle than household, made for the hall with rattling scabbards.

Philippa and Lea listened with abated breath as the sounds from beyond the door seemed to grow distant, as the martial party seemed to leave them. They looked to one another with rising hope that they were safe. Yet, an infant does not know the world's dangers, and he decided upon that moment to bite in first teething. Philippa, in a moment's shock, allowed him to release her, and he made a soft cry of breath.

Monmouth was the last in the room as William hesitated at the door. They both had heard.

"Think you the babe could bolt the door?" Monmouth smiled with dark satisfaction. "Bring me a halberd from the stores."

William hurried from the door to find the tool.

Edward paced in the cellar, in his manner of impatience. There was still no sign. He was torn between waiting and going back up to the stairs with his rusty candle knife. He worried that he had left his wife too long already. He peered again into the pit, dark and still.

"Do not fail me, Richard," he prayed. "Time runs short."

He paced more, questioning all that he had allowed to overtake him. He thought of Philippa, counting upon a young husband, who would be undone by that inexorable drip of time upon which fate turns. If he departed, help might come but would not find him, and if he waited longer, would be too late.

Monmouth swung the ax blade of the halberd against the door to the wardrobe, splintering the wood. He worked as a woodsman at the heavy door as Terplington arrived.

"The king was not in his chamber," said Terplington, observing his effort. "Did you miss the queen?"

Monmouth held his stroke, annoyed with the rebuke—was it not obvious what he was about? "She's sealed within. But this old wood won't stand long."

Terplington nodded, having no time for diplomacy. "We search for the cowardly boy king, then." He paused to remind Monmouth of the object of their mission. "Remember to not harm the child."

Terplington took the two captains with him and departed, leaving Monmouth to continue to hack at the door.

In the cave, Richard tried to pull himself up the slippery rock, which had narrowed to a frightening degree, far more than he remembered on his downward journey. He was jammed in the tiny space, with his sword catching in a crevice. It was pitch black ahead with no sign of any exit. He strained to twist himself free with a pained grunt. Montagu, following at his feet with the torch, called up.

"Is this the familiar passage?"

"I cannot tell! It seemed wider going down!" Richard struggled a bit more. "Perhaps we should try the other."

Montagu, too, was jammed into the narrow tunnel, barely able to turn or free his arm.

"I am cramped with weapons and cannot reverse!" he called above in gallows determination. "If this is not the way, then here we die!"

Edward still paced above, straining with anxiety. He stooped yet again to peer into the black hole. No sign. No sign. He called in a hushed shout.

"Richard?!"

Nothing. The hole was vacant and silent as the grave.

Philippa and Lea clutched together on the cot in the wardrobe as board by board, the halberd blade broke through the door. Philippa tried to soothe her son's now open crying. There was no more hope of deception.

Having weakened the door, Monmouth jabbed the halberd's pole into the jamb and pried, pulling with all his straining might. The door cracked and suddenly shattered open.

Monmouth bulled through the remainder splinters of the destroyed barrier, shoving the piled table and chest aside. Lea leapt up from the cot and rushed to defend her mistress.

"You shall not harm my lady, Devil's Beast!" She struck at him with small fists, but he drew a dagger from his belt and gripped her tightly by one arm, held in a grip so tight that it might snap the frail bone. She struggled in the trap, but could not escape. He sliced the blade of the dagger across the soft, fleshy folds of her throat.

"Silent shrew!" he growled and dropped her to the floor, where blood flowed from the wound in a spreading pool. Philippa cried out in horror at her loyal maid's fate. She had known her as a mother and a friend, that she should pay so much in sacrifice. Yet, she had little time to mourn as her own fate was soon clear.

The two younger Mortimers rushed in past the mountain form of Monmouth and grabbed Philippa, each by an arm, pulling her up. With both arms yanked, she could no longer hold her infant, and the babe fell to the stone floor.

"My child!" she cried out, reaching toward him, but held fast by strong arms.

"Is it broke?" asked Monmouth.

William Mortimer tapped at the baby with his toe. Some straw spread upon the hard schist stone had been the only cushion of its fall. The child wailed in cries of urgent unhappiness.

"'Tis healthy of lung."

"Then leave the royal pup," Monmouth commanded, satisfied at least that it had not been ruined. "Bring the bitch."

"My babe! My babe! My son!" Philippa cried out as she was dragged from the chamber.

The infant prince was left crying on the floor next to the body of Lea, pouring life onto the cold stones as Philippa was torn from the room.

As they dragged Philippa out of her chamber door, she called to Edward, not knowing he was distant below. "Edward! Husband!"

There was no answer.

Edward waited futilely at the hole. There had been no sign of Richard beyond some faint distant murmur, which could have been but a wind in the cave or a falling stone. He could now hear the faint cries of Philippa's voice calling his name, drifting down from spiraling stairs above. He could wait no longer.

"Oh, Richard, you have failed me and damned me," he said with loss of last hope, considering the small knife gripped in his hand, vowing to himself, "If Edward must fall in honor of his Lady, he'll take as many with him as God may grant."

He turned at last, away from the rotting hole, and started up the steps to meet his fate.

Terplington and the two captains hurried through the castle from hall to hall and throwing open any door that might conceal the hiding place of the young king.

"The coward prince hides, even at the sacrifice of his lady love," was Terplington's curse as they searched. "He cannot tremble in secret for long, lest he wallow in his own piss in some cupboard."

As they strode down the corridor toward the stair passage from below, Edward crouched in the shadows, hearing them coming, gripping the knife. He prepared himself for attack, outnumbered against soldiers with swords, but at the entrance to the gallery where he waited, Terplington sent the captains at opposite split to the upper chambers again.

After they had gone, Edward prepared to follow, hoping he might have the advantage of surprise and might take a sword from one of them. He raised himself to leave his concealment, but then heard the moan of what seemed faint voices, and a muffled clatter of arms. He was unsure from whence it came. He listened in silent care, then, with a sudden rise of hope, turned to the hidden stair from which he had come. He heard again.

Edward returned, hurrying back down the spiral into the croft of wine barrels. He ran to the hole and peered in. There seemed to be a faint glimmer of some flickering light from the darkness below. He shoved a burning taper into the opening mouth of the grotto, just catching the glimmer of the buckle of a sword girth, and then Richard's face peering from the stony confines. His heart leapt with the return of hope.

"Sir Friend, you cut me close. But I'll make you Chancellor if you've brought other friends," he said with a wishful mirth, holding his relief in the balance.

Richard handed up Lancaster's sword.

"Take this for friendship from Lancaster, and God's wounds, give me a hand from this hellish pit! Montagu follows."

Edward extended a hand into the abyss and Richard grasped it, pulling up out of the hole.

Then, Montagu soon appeared, then Rokeby and the others, one by one.

The loyal men, seven in number, gathered in the croft for Edward to apprise of the state of their position, but urged them that there was little time to plan. Some argued they might break open the gates from within that more might come to their aid, but Edward warned they had no time for more.

"They have my queen and we cannot wait for better," Edward said. "If we arouse alarm, we might be trapped. Mortimer plans in my mother's apartments. We must surprise them."

Montagu agreed, and they quickly made their way up the spiraling steps.

As they emerged into the gallery, and all was silent, Montagu tried to get to the front of Edward that he might lead.

"My Liege, it be safer if you followed."

Yet, Edward, held at bay for too long, would not be moved aside. "I have left my crown too long in the grasp of others. If I cannot defend it now, I have no right to it." And he hurried away down the corridor with the rest following, trying to keep up.

Monmouth and the two Mortimer sons dragged the struggling Philippa with hands over her mouth into the chamber where Mortimer waited at the end of the table.

"Terplington searches for the king who skulks about the castle in fear," Monmouth reported.

"Then ungag the lady. Her cries may bring him from hiding."

The sons took their hands from Philippa's mouth, but she didn't scream. She only fixed Mortimer with a cold, defiant glare. "Do with me, sir, as your heart cares. I will not cry out."

"Let us use her each in turn, Father," said William Mortimer, gripping her throat in his hand, "We will stop her pride."

She spat in the son's face, so that her own fear might not show, bracing herself for what might follow, and damning it, "If the father will come nearer, he may receive my blessing as well."

The two Mortimer sons hoisted Philippa up and slammed her on her back on top of the map of England spread upon the table.

"Let her receive your blessing then, Father," grinned Henry, "before we open her up with sharp steel."

Philippa trembled as Mortimer leaned over the table, looking into her face. He took her chin tightly in his hand, stroking a finger on her soft lips.

"Does my proud lady still seek to refuse Mortimer what is his by right of ancestry?" he crooned in oblique and maddening puzzle.

"What does he claim by ancestry, beyond his evil-eye?" she asked in perilous challenge, young and innocent against aged corruption, hoping for any delay of what she knew would surely come.

"Why, all that is the Plantagenets' should rightfully belong to the name Mortimer." He leaned over her, that she might look into his stern and triumphant face. "All that was usurped by William called Conqueror from my own progenitor should, by God's right, come to me—crown, lands, wife. All. For forty years I have worked to this end. And you," he smiled, "will deny me?"

Philippa was still and silent as he revealed his true heart. His face before her was like a map of avarice and envy, and she reflected in his black eye.

"You tremble at my discolored orb. From my father, I received my strength of arm, and from my mother who killed him, I received affliction." Mortimer's father indeed had been struck to death by the blade of a jealous wife of hot Spanish temper, betrothed by distance for gain of position, and herself imprisoned for madness. "Such is the legacy parents leave their children. My sons will have a kingdom."

Philippa had heard all of Mortimer's history from dead Lea's gossip, and now she knew his intent. If Edward were to die and his princely son placed on the throne and proclaimed king, as Edward had replaced his own father, Mortimer and Isabella might rule without hindrance. And should the infant king die without clear a successor, for surely the weak-lunged young brother could easily succumb, Mortimer could seize the crown for himself. He would end the reign of the Plantagenets, with no allegiance to the charter signed by the discredited John of that name, and make himself dictator, as Caesar had replaced Rome. She could see all outlined in the map of his darkly satisfied countenance.

Edward led the band of loyal swords through passages he knew as quickly as secrecy could allow, but they could not move with total silence. They soon came face to face with Terplington and the captains. Surprise had taken them within fathoms of their goal. They drew swords.

In the chamber, the clang of swords echoed from the passageways.

Monmouth turned at the noise, his hand moving to the hilt of his sword. "The sounds of struggle, my lord."

Yet, Mortimer did not take his gaze from Philippa.

"Could it be the boy puts up a last fight?" he smirked, not believing it more than a nuisance. "What says my lady to Mortimer's suit? If she consents freely to his will, he shall let her live to old age in a safe convent."

Philippa stared deep into his black eye, and spat in it.

Edward's men fought the two captains while Montagu battled Terplington. The swords were close in the narrow confines. Montagu finally thrust his sword into Terplington's gut. The knight stumbled and dropped to a knee, his entrails spilling into his hand.

"For Beaumont and Kent!" Montagu shouted, in satisfied revenge.

Yet, the fight was not won. Richard battled one of the captains and thrust his sword under his arm, mortally wounding him. The other captain, left without defense, dropped his sword and surrendered.

"Mercy, my Liege," he cried out. Montagu would have struck off his head, but Edward stayed him. He hurried on down the corridor without waiting for the others.

Montagu looked to Richard, "My lord is still hasty in his passions." Then to the others, "Follow the king!"

It was only when Mortimer and the others heard the rush of footsteps outside the door they realized.

"To the door!" Monmouth shouted. He and Henry Mortimer leapt to the door to try to block it, but the men outside pounced against it.

Isabella came from her chamber at the commotion in an untied bed shift, barely covering her nakedness. She could only stand to watch as they wrestled on either side, teetering on the brink.

There were more men outside than in, and they finally shoved the barrier door open with a shout. Montagu and Richard were first in. Edward started to follow but saw his mother in undress and was frozen to the spot.

Monmouth jumped to battle, but Montagu, swift and furious, thrust his sword into the large target of Monmouth's breast and into his heart. The dark and powerful knight was held for a moment upon his toes, until a crimson flow of blood burst from his mouth. He fell to the floor stones like a tree.

Edward stepped back from the door, unable to face the vision of his mother, closing his eyes painfully as she called out to him.

"Juste fil, Edward! My son, have pity on my gentle Mortimer!"

Taking a breath, he finally launched into the room.

The two Mortimer sons, seeing the mighty Monmouth felled, dropped their swords and fell to their knees with clasped hands.

"Mercy, Sire!" Henry, the younger, pleaded.

His brother, William, who had much hand in the plot, turned upon his progenitor to save his own skin, "Judge us not by the deeds of our father," he cried, "Mercy on us!

Mortimer, now alone, stood upon the far side of the table. Released from his hold, Philippa ran to Edward's arms. He comforted her, holding her tight and feeling her tremble, his own heart pounding that he had nearly been too late. Seeing she was safe, he stepped toward Mortimer with his sword leveled.

Mortimer stood tall as pride would allow him. "You seek vengeance on Mortimer? You will not have it." He quickly pulled a dagger from his belt and tried to thrust it into his own throat. Montagu's men leapt to grasp him, to keep him from killing himself, holding him for Edward to strike.

"Thrust a sword into this black traitor's heart, now, my Liege. We here are jury. There," he gestured to the map spread upon the table, "is the evidence."

Edward held his sword ready, prepared to strike, with the rising emotion in his heart for all Mortimer had been to him and betrayed, the murders of his father and uncle, and intent to murder him and his own family. Yet, had he not been the champion of justice? Had he not set the rule of impartial judges that might decide upon guilt? Had he not sworn to the Charter? And so, he might have ended it, yet he hesitated.

"I will have my enemy judged," Edward said. "His fate will come in the Tower, with trial, as it rightly should have been."

Suddenly, Mortimer lurched and turned the dagger blade and stabbed it into the spleen of one of Montagu's men. He grabbed his sword, and with a growl, thrust it into the neck of the other. His sons grasped up their swords and dashed from the room.

Mortimer, with sword held at point, backed from the room with Montagu and the others held at bay.

"The tower to hold me has not yet been built, young prince."

And so he vanished from the room.

Isabella rushed to follow, but Montagu held her. She shouted after her paramour, "Roger! Gentile Mortimer! My love! Abandon not Isabel!" No longer the wolf queen, but a woman in a night shift, she cried, turning her eyes to her son for pity. "Do not harm him."

Mortimer and his sons dashed through the castle. They found their way down into the lower gallery, looking for escape. Here, they spotted the monk confessor coming from the cellar. When he saw the look in Mortimer's black eye, he ran back to the entrance.

"Follow!" shouted Mortimer, and the sons rushed to keep the monk from securing the door. He ran down the steps as quickly as his old legs would take him.

William and Henry clattered quickly down the steps, with their father following. They found the monk as he struggled to conceal the hole with the cask. William Mortimer fell upon him and struck the confessor with his sword, sending him bleeding against the foundation rock.

"The hole, Father!" Henry pulled at the barrel to free the entrance. "Must be how they gained the castle."

William helped him to topple the barrel, spilling the musty liquid contents in a flood which doused the fallen monk's body with the thick red of the fruit mixing with his blood. An old crusader, it seemed sent on to the left hand of the God he served.

Mortimer made to enter the tunnel for escape, turning to his sons to follow. "To the battlefield, then."

~~~

CHAPTER TEN

1

20th Day of November, 1330

The rays of the rising dawn sun elongated across the fields of Nottingham, glinting on the armor of knights arrayed in a line of battle, in advance of rows of archers.

Mortimer's men, called by William from near station at Beeston, were aligned on one side of the plain. Edward's loyal lords and knights were gathered on the other, Montagu's modest force and Lancaster's, Earl Warwick, and Suffolk's, outnumbered as they were arrayed against the former camp tents. Smoke from doused campfires drifted in the blowing wind, mixing with the cloying mist of the foggy field, so that true numbers could not be counted.

Mortimer had dressed in armor and was mounted atop a great black horse, flanked by his armored sons, knights that Edward had blessed with his own sword, prepared to tear him down.

Edward, in armor with his red and blue colors of the "lions and the lis", mixing the houses of his Plantagenet ancestors, and his mother's claim to the French kingdom, sat astride a grey stallion, holding it from prancing with his own roiling energy. Montagu,
264

Richard, and old Lancaster sat astride just behind him, looking across the battlefield.

The forces were all hastily gathered. Many of Mortimer's soldiers of pike and ax were Welshmen conscripted from the wild lands across the march, who held the English crown with small love.

Lancaster, the old soldier, whose eyes could only see shades at distance, but whose ears could count the breath of men and rattle of arms from across the fields, offered counsel to the young king whom he had placed to guard the realm and supported. He knew the truth of their circumstance. They had slowed Mortimer's plot, but were still at mortal disadvantage.

"Their surprise may be lost, Edward, but they have us fair by number. Our archers are few and ragged. But they will account themselves, even unto slaughter."

Edward turned his horse to the scrawny number of his own side. He turned back to look at Mortimer across the field and the bristling arms behind him, glinting through the mist. He searched his soul for guidance and thought of his confessors, who had sacrificed themselves for him. He thought of all that he had confessed. He looked at the old Earl with failing eyes, peering into the mists, prepared that it would be the last of earth he would see.

"Then I will not have them slaughtered for my own failure of vision," he said with a certainty of his conviction. "If I believe in the laws of chivalry, and put my faith in the true justice of my God, I will face my enemy. For I have brought us to this."

He spurred his horse, riding out into the center of the field to the shock and amazement of his own men, and of Mortimer's followers across the field. Reaching the center point between opposing sides, he rose in his stirrups, calling out in a clear voice that all to the lowest man might hear him.

"Men of the March and you of Wales, and my disaffected lords who would follow this man I once called friend—let us save bloodshed. My lord Mortimer claims right to my crown. Let him come forth and take it by his own sword on the field of combat—if he is able."

The soldiers and knights across the field waited in anxious curiosity at this turn, for it seemed mad to them. This young king had been rumored to quick temper and rash act. Could this be evidence? Yet, here he was before them, alone on the field.

A Welsh archer drew his bow as if to loose an arrow, but one of the knights on horse gestured with his gauntleted hand to stay. This boy king he had also known in battle, when he had called upon all who followed him to the code they had vowed to serve. It was rare in the practice of their lives for the vaunted nobles of high position to practice what they swore, but before him now was one, by example, all he claimed to believe.

Mortimer rode forward on his black animal to meet him on the field. His sons rode out with him, flanking him, but holding a bit behind.

Montagu held his ground that he might not set the host at war. He turned to Richard beside him, marveling even at the young king's will, but doubting Mortimer.

"Brave he is. But what treachery lies ahead, I cannot say."

Mortimer reined his horse up before Edward, the colors hanging from his animal snapping in the wind. They were familiar with one another in temperament, old friends turned to open adversaries. Mortimer knew that it was his pride which placed the boy in such witless position, and not justice.

"You feel ready to have me, then, young prince?" he challenged the young man, no longer boy.

"You'll find my sword is no stick of wood," Edward answered. "Let God decide."

"Well, then, have on!" Mortimer drew his sword in a flash and swung the heavy blade. Edward barely managed to draw his in time to meet it.

Mortimer turned his horse for better advantage and Edward was just able to slip his shield from the saddle hook onto his arm, blocking another powerful blow. The fight was on in earnest, young king and seasoned warrior, sword to sword, horse to horse, in single combat on the field of men, held by a sliver of chance. Edward seemed to hold his own against the skilled knight.

Mortimer spun away from a swing by Edward and, at advantage again, thrust his sword into the flank of Edward's horse. The horse crumpled, dying under Edward's mount, tossing him to the ground, trapping him partly underneath.

Edward struggled to free his leg, trapped by the animal's barding armor. The two Mortimer sons now charged forward, intent that they would finish him, bearing down on him with their swords at once. Edward flung his shield, catching William in the throat, throwing him back from the saddle to the earth. He ducked the close swiping blade of Henry's sword as he made a pass.

Richard started to spur his horse to even the odds, but Montagu held him back.

"If we enter the field, hell and butchery follow," Montagu cautioned. "The king is at his word." Richard restrained himself, in an agony of frustration that he could not interfere.

Edward was just able to pull himself free from the horse as William was rising from the grassy, muddy, dew and rain wet ground. As he reached for his sword upon the earth, Edward swung his and hacked a wound deep into the mail of William's arm.

William cried out, holding his wound, but facing the look in Edward's eye, lurched away from the fight.

Mortimer watched his son scurrying across the field back toward the battle line. Edward stood his ground between the two knights on horse.

Mortimer waved Henry back and swung himself from his horse to the ground, striding at Edward with his heavy Claymore.

Edward and Mortimer dueled in the mud of the field, sword upon sword and shield, steel boots mixing the earth with the blood of Edward's horse and of Mortimer's son. Blow upon blow, faint and parry, until Mortimer's heavy sword struck Edward square and threw him backward onto the ground.

Edward lay in the muck, seeming to have lost his sword. Mortimer took advantage and raised his sword high against the grey-clouded sky to strike an execution blow.

"For my father—!" he roared, but as he swung the blade, Edward pulled his hand from deep in the muck, still gripping his sword, bringing up the blade dripping with mud and blood, and thrust it into Mortimer's thigh.

Mortimer cried out at the wound, stumbling upon his footing and sinking to the ground, his heavy sword falling from his hand. As he tried to rise again, Edward stood and thrust the point of the sword further through his flesh and muscle, into the earth, pinning his leg to the spot.

With a cry of rage, Henry Mortimer charged forward on his horse, raising his sword to strike. As he came on, Edward grabbed up Mortimer's Claymore, and swung the long blade with two hands. The heavy blade sliced clean through Henry's torso as he passed. One half of the body fell into the mud and the other half was carried off on the horse, feet still in the stirrups, in a ghostly ride.

Edward drew his own sword from Mortimer's leg. Mortimer cried out in anguish, not from his wound but from his hacked son lying near him, still dying.

Edward stood over Mortimer, holding the tip of his sword to his throat, victor, but without triumph.

"The point is settled, Mortimer of Wigmore. Father for son—" he looked to Henry, whose glistening eyes, still searching for life and body, finally faded. "Son for father."

Edward turned to the knights and soldiers on the enemy side, shouting that all might hear.

"My lords, as equals, who grant me the rights I hold, as I hope to be fair in justice as I swore at Westminster, he will be given benefit of trial by jury of peers. Let us live by laws, and their judgment will be as it may."

A murmur of approval spread through the knights. And he turned to the men-at-arms behind them, who knew no privileges of their rank, but hoped that justice might be theirs too.

"And to you of the Welsh lands—Siaradaf â chi, da a ffyddlon," he spoke in their own tongue, that they might hear him as well.

"My grandfather promised you a prince who would speak a familiar language in court so he could hear your grievances. In my father you had disappointment—as did I. I now have an infant son who will grow to manhood in a land where from this day forward English will be our common language, not the Normandy tongue of my forebears. And from this day hence, the firstborn son of England's king will be a Prince of Wales. Join with me as one common people," he urged with an honest heart, hoping that he had been heard, "or draw your bows and slay me where I stand."

A hushed silence fell across the field, with only the wind whipping the tent flaps and a soft clatter of arrow quivers in the ranks. Montagu and Lancaster, Richard and Rokeby, watched and waited for what might follow.

Then, all the knights on both sides dismounted their horses and dropped to a knee. The archers and pikemen followed, until a sea of armed warriors knelt as one in the foggy mists of Nottingham wood. The knights clapped armored gauntlets to their breastplates.

"For Edward!" they shouted, with a cry of acclamation. "Long live the King!" echoed across the field.

Montagu and Richard joined Edward, clapping him upon the shoulder in cheer and congratulation. Yet, Edward turned to look back toward the wall of the castle, lofty and dark shrouded above.

High on the battlement, Isabella stood between yeoman guards, still undressed, in her nightgown and bare feet, looking down on her son and her fallen lover.

Montagu followed Edward's gaze.

"And what of the Queen, your mother?" he asked. "Does she not share Mortimer's state?"

"I will not shame her at public trial," was his reply.

Isabella, at last, pulled her sheer gown close against the breeze and turned away.

"But she will spend the rest of her days in Kenilworth, where she may have comfort, and visit of her children, but cannot plot, nor raise armies. And where my father found his last quiet days with his poems."

2

29th Day of November, 1330

Mortimer stood on a wooden scaffold built on the soft ground before the rising four corners of the Tower, hands bound, as Lancaster read from a parchment, held close to his face. A host of hundreds had gathered after the trial to witness the payment of his deeds.

"Roger Mortimer, Lord of Wigmore, Denbigh and Clun, you are found guilty of Treason by High Crime and Misdemeanor. That you did seek to injure the King, did cause to be murdered Edward of Caernarfon, did illegally cause to be executed the Earl of Kent, did by deceit, frustrate the King's actions against the Scots and force an unjust peace for personal gain, did under false pretense lead men-at-arms against Lancaster and cause the death of Sir John Beaumont."

As Lancaster read the indictment, Mortimer listened in silence, looking up at the birds flying through the clouded air. As he watched, a kestrel dropped from the clouds and struck upon a gull, carrying the prey off to its fate, as Mortimer would be carried to his. The sky was reflected in his eye, darker than the other.

"Sentence passed," continued Lancaster, "to be carried out on morn of Thursday, Twenty-Ninth Day of

November, Thirteen Hundred and Thirtieth Year of Our Lord, that you be hung by the neck, your entrails thrown to the wind, and your head shall be removed to be posted on London Bridge as warning to all others who may seek to follow in your path."

The heavy sentence was visited upon the accused in all its horrible ceremony and soon, the eye was glossy and visible to all as it looked out with empty soul from its pole upon the bridge of London. The commoners and tradesmen, who busied themselves at their stalls upon the bridge, could look upon it as they lived their lives, in a land now at peace.

A boat passed underneath the bridge, of royal state, with a black sash across the colors, rowed by strong arms up the swirling stream. Upon the deck was Isabella, once the queen of legendary beauty and strength of will who turned the fate of a kingdom, in her rich dressing of expensive cloth, but arms bound by rope, that she may not escape, nor throw herself to harm in the water. She looked up to the once handsome head rising from the bridge bulwark upon the pole, its familiar features now twisted and amassed with flies. And still she loved him.

Lancaster stood upon the bridge, near death himself, looking up at Mortimer's head and then watching Isabella barging up the river. He turned away, supported by an attendant.

Edward had bid farewell to his mother, and joined with his wife, holding their infant prince, Edward, in their arms.

~~~

EPILOGUE

Geoffrey Chaucer sat thoughtfully quiet a moment, then looked up into his audience's eyes as shades of eve began to cloak them in shadow, but still held in rapt enthrall, some of them dewy with tears, but whether of satisfaction or sorrow could not be told.

"And so, the boy had at last come to be ruler of himself," the storyteller said, with his own musing. "And our great Edward has ruled for these fifty years with beloved Queen Philippa at his side. I have served them both."

He looked back to the doors of the great church where the line of mourners had still filed within for the full day and into night.

"It is said he has died of grief at her passing these short years ago."

The merchant's son stepped forward to speak up in brave questioning, "Kind sir, is all you have told us the truth? These events seem too fantastic."

Chaucer broke a gentle smile of amusement and teasingly tousled the boy's hair.

"Save for a few embellishments of the storyteller's art, I swear my tale was the true shape of it."

The wheelwright spoke loudly from the back of the gathered. He was aged enough that he knew some of this tale. "I have heard that Mortimer's unsaved spirit still walks the battlements of the Tower."

Chaucer shrugged. "These things are for others to say. His remains were buried in an unmarked grave. And as for the passionate young king, our good Edward, his Order of The Knights of the Garter, a boastful promise of youth he fulfilled in due course of time, continues today as a symbol of noble ideals too easily forgotten."

Then, he gestured his listeners closer, conspiratorially whispering aloud, that they might be held by suspense of further secrets.

"I could tell how our young Edward later secreted himself into France disguised as a beggar under threat of death by the French King, and very nearly united the two kingdoms under one flag—"

He held his thought, leaning back upon the step, pleased by their breathless interest. "But that, as we might say—is another story."

Within the cathedral, as mourners filed past the great stone carved tomb where images of aged Edward and Philippa rested side by side, under a stone relief emblem of the Order of The Garter, a motto was cast in the stone, "Honi Soit Qui Mal Y Pense" (Shame on any who think ill of it!), and a tattered strip of soiled silk dangled from it, tickled by the unseen breeze from the open doors.

❖

Author Michael January

Michael January is a writer for film and television as well as a travel writer and photographer. His "Favorite Castles" book series is in its fourth edition with "Favorite Castles of Germany" and "Favorite Castles of Switzerland" as well as England & Wales and the "Favorite Castles of Ireland". This is his third historical novel. "The Secret Memoirs of Mary Shelley: The Frankenstein Diaries" and "Aces: A Novel of Pilots in WWII" are available in print, ebook and audiobook.

If you enjoyed The Boy King's Tale,
please kindly leave a review at your
favorite book site, or tell a friend.

MichaelJanuaryAuthor.com

Amazon Author Page
amazon.com/Michael-January/e/B00CJNK16O/

Facebook
facebook.com/michaeljanuaryauthor/

WingedLionPublications.com

Ingram Content Group UK Ltd.
Milton Keynes UK
UKHW020653270623
424112UK00014B/427